This book belongs to

Stories were specially written for this book by:

Georgina Adams Elizabeth Cooper Janice Godfrey
Gillian Maxwell Ralph Whitlock

The illustrations are by:

Grahame Corbett Anna Dzierzek Douglas Hall Nina Klein
Anthony Morris Cheryl Pelavin Rosamund Pickless Joanna Ross
Alan Saunders Lesley Smith Joanna Stubbs

The cover illustration is by Carol Lawson

Some of the stories and illustrations in this book first
appeared in annuals and storybooks published by The Hamlyn
Publishing Group between 1963 and 1971.

Published 1976 by
The Hamlyn Publishing Group Limited
London · New York · Sydney · Toronto
Astronaut House, Feltham, Middlesex, England
© Copyright 1976 by the Hamlyn Publishing Group Limited

ISBN 0 600 30313 6

Printed by New Interlitho, Milan, Italy.

My Animal Storybook

HAMLYN
London · New York · Sydney · Toronto

Contents

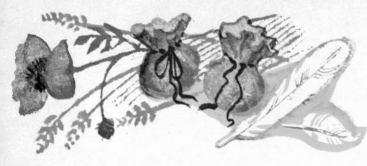

Shoes for Geese

A long time ago, there lived a goose girl called Maisie. In spring, when the little fluffy goslings were big enough, she used to take them with their mothers and fathers out to the common to eat the grass. The little goslings were soon nearly as big as their parents and covered with feathers instead of down.

Early in September, Maisie used to set out for her summer holiday in the big city. This was quite an adventure for her, as the city was a long, long way away. But when Maisie was a girl there were no trains or buses or cars. So Maisie had to walk. All the way to the city and all the way back again.

Her father went with her, and so did the geese – hundreds and hundreds of them! For her father's job was to take all the geese he could collect from surrounding farms to market in the city. And they had to walk, too.

Early one morning, after breakfast, Maisie and her father and Dumper the dog gathered all the geese together and started on their journey. They walked slowly, with the geese wandering all over the countryside, looking for food. Geese like to eat grass and insects and seeds, but they need time to look for their food. Maisie and her father and Dumper the dog never tried to hurry them and the geese were very contented.

That night they all slept in a farmyard. The geese sat down in a big yard, with Dumper to protect them against the foxes. Maisie and her father curled up on a big pile of hay in the barn.

Maisie's father went the same way every year, and so he knew all the farmers along the road and where he would spend each night. The farmers were all glad to see him, and some of them sold him more geese. So the goose flock kept increasing.

September is harvest-time. So the farther they went, the more corn-fields they found harvested. Then the geese were allowed to roam over the stubbles and pick up all the stray grains of corn. They became very fat.

Although they walked mostly over grass tracks, they got tired, walking every day, and some of them became lame.

In a little town on the way there lived a kind old shoemaker. Maisie and her father used to take their shoes to him to be mended. One day, Maisie went into

his workshop carrying a goose under each arm.

'What's the trouble?' asked the shoemaker, whose name was John Penty.

'They're lame,' said Maisie. 'They've been walking so far, their feet are sore.'

'Well, well,' said Mr Penty. 'We must see what we can do about that. Leave them with me and come back at four o'clock.'

And when Maisie went back, each goose had little shoes of soft leather on their feet. The shoes were tied with a lace around their legs. They looked really smart. And the geese stalked out of the workshop as proudly as queens wearing crowns on their head. They liked their brand-new shoes.

From then on, John Penty made shoes for all the geese which happened to be lame when Maisie and her father arrived at his town.

He put a notice in his workshop window. It said:

John Penty, Shoemaker for Geese.

9

The Mouse
with Long Whiskers

Once upon a time, there was a little grey mouse called Whiskers. His whiskers were so long that he had to tie them behind his head in a bow so that he would not trip over them.

All the other mice thought it was very funny to see a mouse with his whiskers tied behind his head in a big, red bow. Whiskers was very sad because everybody laughed at him.

One day he was nibbling on a piece of cheese at his kitchen table, when he heard a knock on his front door. When he opened it, there, on his doorstep, were three policemice.

Whiskers had such a fright when he saw them that he nearly choked on his cheese. He could not think of anything he had done wrong.

'Wh-What do you want?' he asked in a shaky voice.

'Don't be afraid,' replied one of the policemice. 'We have come to see if you can help us.'

'Me! Help you! How?' asked Whiskers, very surprised.

'Well,' said another policemouse, 'little Micky Curlytail has fallen down a big hole and can't get out again. He is crying and very frightened.'

'But what can I do to help?' asked the little mouse.

'Lend us your whiskers,' said the third policemouse.

'My whiskers! But they won't be any help. People only laugh at them,' said Whiskers.

'Come with us and we'll show you,' said the first policemouse.

So Whiskers put on his little red coat and went with the three policemice.

They walked a little way until they came to a crowd of very excited mice, all standing around the edge of a large hole.

The policemice told everyone to move back and pushed Whiskers to the edge of the hole.

Whiskers looked over the edge and there at the bottom of the hole, crying and making a terrible fuss, was Micky Curlytail. Whiskers felt very sorry for him. 'What can I do?' he asked.

'Untie your whiskers,' said one of the policemice, 'and let them drop down the hole. Then Micky will tie them around his waist and you can pull him out, with some help from us.'

'What a good idea!' said Whiskers. He immediately undid the bow that tied his whiskers, and let them drop down the hole.

'Tie them around your waist, Micky,' he called. So Micky did.

'Hold tight,' said Whiskers.

'Yes, I will,' replied Micky, who had stopped crying.

'Now, I'm going to pull you out. Stand back everybody.'

So everybody stood back and the three policemice held on to Whiskers' coat-tails. They all pulled and puffed. Slowly but surely they lifted Micky out of the hole. When he got to the top, Mrs Curlytail rushed over and hugged Micky. Then she kissed Whiskers, which made him turn as pink in the face as a pink sugar mouse.

'Thank you, Whiskers,' she cried. 'I'm sorry for laughing at your long whiskers, and I'll never laugh at you again.'

All the mice carried Whiskers off on their shoulders, cheering loudly and saying what a clever mouse he was.

Whiskers the mouse never felt unhappy about his long whiskers again. He was treated as a hero in mouseland and everybody loved him. Some of the mice even tried to grow whiskers as long as his, but they never could.

Curious Christabel

Sally, the grey Persian cat, had four little kittens and they all lived with a little girl named Jane. Once the kittens were old enough, Sally did not mind Jane stroking them.

Three of the kittens were just like Sally. They were little balls of silky, grey fluff, and they had blue eyes. But the fourth one was black and white and had a short, sleek coat. She was not as pretty as her brothers and sister. She had a face patched black and white, which made her look like a clown.

'We must give her a very pretty name, then she won't mind looking different,' Jane said to Sally. 'Christabel is a nice name, isn't it?'

As time went on, the three pretty kittens went to new homes. Jane's friends all wanted the fluffy, grey kittens, but nobody seemed to want to take Christabel. So she stayed at home with Sally and Jane.

Christabel was a playful little kitten, but she was also very curious. Sally had to scold Christabel often.

'You must not be so curious!' she would say. 'Something unpleasant may happen to you one day.'

One afternoon Jane's mother finished her ironing and went upstairs to put the clean clothes away. She opened a drawer in Jane's room and had partly filled it, when the telephone rang. She shut the drawer quickly and went downstairs to answer the telephone. She did not know that curious Christabel had crept into the drawer!

The time went by and it was dark and stuffy in the drawer. Christabel miaowed very loudly.

Sally and Jane were both busily looking for Christabel. Jane was quite late going to bed, and she was very sad when her mother said they would have to wait until morning to see if Christabel had come home. But when she was undressed and everything was quiet, she heard Christabel crying. She opened the drawer and there was the missing kitten! Christabel was very pleased to see her.

'I hope this will cure your curiosity,' said Sally sternly to her kitten.

Christabel simply said, 'Yes, Mamma.' And this time it did!

Matthew's New Home

Matthew Mouse lived in a hole in the attic of an old house. He had lived there for a long time, and he was very happy. Then, one day, a cat called Charlie came to live in the house. Matthew did not like cats, and he ran away as fast as he could, out of the house and through the town until he reached a wood. Matthew stopped to rest and to think about what he would do next. Suddenly, he noticed an old, blue teapot lying in some grass nearby, and he thought it would make a splendid new home for him. He was just hurrying towards it, when Jeremy Robin flew down beside him.

'Where are you going?' asked Jeremy.

'I'm going to make that teapot my home,' said Matthew.

'But it's my home!' said Jeremy. 'I've built my nest inside it.'

'Oh!' said Matthew, feeling very disappointed. 'It would have made a lovely home.'

He turned and walked away. He would just have to find somewhere else to live.

'But where?' he wondered.

Jeremy thought very hard for a while, and then he flew after Matthew, calling, 'Wait Wait! I have an idea.'

Jeremy soon explained to Matthew that he saw no reason why they shouldn't *both* live in the teapot!

'There's plenty of room in the spout,' said Jeremy. 'You would be warm and cosy in there, and you could listen to me singing.'

Matthew thought that was a splendid idea, and they hurried back to the old teapot. Matthew climbed into the spout. He liked it in there so much that he *did* make it his new home. In fact, Matthew Mouse stayed there with Jeremy Robin for years and years and years.

13

The Playful Dolphin

Jolly the dolphin splashed happily through the sea. He was on his way to King Neptune's cave, far, far below the waves. He liked visiting his mermaid friends there, but they were not always pleased to see him, especially when they were busy looking after all the baby mermaids.

Jolly was a playful fellow, always bobbing about, and splashing and playing tricks, and he sometimes got in the mermaids' way. He didn't mean to be a nuisance, but today the mermaids were annoyed with him.

'Jolly, go away! We are busy giving the babies their swimming lesson.'

Jolly did go away, but he soon came back, and when he bobbed up right in the middle of the swimming school, the mermaids were not pleased with him.

'You've upset the babies. Go away!' they said crossly.

'Oh well, I'll come back later,' sighed Jolly, as he swam away.

When he came back, the babies were having their hair washed. Jolly took a sniff at the soap, and it made him sneeze. As he sneezed, he blew soap bubbles all over the cave. The soap bubbles landed on the mermaids' noses and soon everyone was sneezing.

King Neptune left his throne and came to see what all the noise was about.

'It's Jolly,' explained the Chief Mermaid. 'First he spoilt the babies' swimming lesson, and now he's making everyone sneeze.'

'Off you go, Jolly, and find something useful to do,' said King Neptune sternly.

Jolly knew that everyone obeyed the King, so he hurried away at once. But he could not think of anything useful to do. So, he went for a long swim to the beach where he liked to watch the girls and boys playing together.

Today, the girls and boys were playing with a big rubber toy which was filled with air, and shaped like a dolphin. It floated on the sea, and several children could sit on it at once. A grown-up pulled the toy dolphin along by a rope so that he bounced across the waves. How the children enjoyed their ride!

Suddenly, Jolly had a wonderful idea, and he hurried back to King Neptune's cave as fast as he could. Hair-washing time was over now, and the mermaids were busy trying to clean the cave.

'Do be quiet while we work,' they said crossly to their babies.

But the babies just giggled naughtily.

When Jolly appeared, the mermaids sighed, 'Not you as well, Jolly. It's bad enough trying to keep the babies out of our way. We don't want you splashing and diving around us . . .'

'Don't be cross with me. Listen to what I have to say,' replied Jolly. 'I've come to help you. I'm going to take the babies for a ride on my back.'

The mermaids were delighted and they lifted the babies on to Jolly's back.

'Hold tight,' he told the babies.

Then he bobbed up through the waves, and splashed about gently on the surface of the sea, in and out of the rocks. The babies loved the ride, and the mermaids were able to get on with their work in the cave far below. When they had finished, they came up to the top of the sea, to watch Jolly and the babies having fun.

'Will you take us for a ride every day, dear Jolly?' asked the babies.

Of course, Jolly said he would. Now he was being useful *and* having fun.

Abigail and Silas
Talk to the Animals

'I think we'll go to the zoo today,' said Father. 'I'm sure the animals will be pleased to see us.' So he and Silas and Abigail all jumped into a taxi and went off to the zoo.

'I want to climb a tree,' shouted Silas as soon as he saw the first cage.

'Not in my cage,' scowled the baboon, 'and please don't shout so early in the morning.' He had been wakened from his after-breakfast nap, and he was very cross indeed.

'Come and look here,' cried Abigail. 'I've found a cow with funny horns.'

'I'm not a cow, you silly thing,' smiled the animal. 'I'm an elk, and my horns are called antlers.'

'I think we should be polite to this fellow,' whispered Silas to Abigail. 'Good morning, sir,' he said courteously to the polar bear. 'My name is Silas and this is Abigail.'

'Good morning, Silas and Abigail,' replied the polar bear. 'My name is Peter, and this is my friend Richard the racoon, who has dropped in for a chat.'

They all talked together for a few moments, until suddenly they were interrupted by a noisy barking. 'Oh, it's Sinbad the seal again,' sighed Peter. 'I expect he's hungry. He's *always* hungry.'

Sinbad was perched on his stool, with a table napkin around his chin, waving his flippers and calling loudly for his lunch of tasty fish.

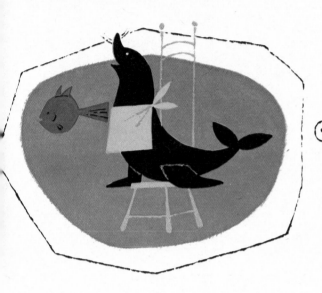

'I'm a bit hungry, too,' said Silas, gazing longingly at an icecream shop . . .

After their icecreams, Abigail and Silas skipped over to see a penguin, who was standing beside a big animal.

'Ladies and Gentlemen, this is my friend the moose,' called the penguin, pointing towards the moose.

'You have much bigger antlers than the elk,' declared Abigail admiringly.

'Of course I have,' said the moose proudly. 'I'm much bigger than the elk, and much finer!'

Next, Silas and Abigail walked over to pay their respects to the lions, who were just finishing their afternoon meal. 'I'm very tired,' yawned the big father lion. 'It's been a long day.'

'It certainly has,' agreed Abigail sleepily, as Father took them by the hand and led them towards the main gate. On the way out, they waved goodbye to all the animals and said how much they had liked visiting them.

'I can't decide which animal I liked best,' declared Abigail. 'We'll just have to pay them another visit soon, so that I can make up my mind.'

The Lost Star

Fairy Twinkle put on her best dress. The jewels round the skirt twinkled like tiny stars as she danced for joy.

'Hurry,' cried her friends, Sparkle and Gleam, 'we must not be late for the Fairy Queen's Birthday Ball.'

Soon the moonlit sky was filled with the flutter of fairy wings and excited whisperings.

Suddenly, below them, the fairies saw the golden towers of the palace. But, what was wrong?

Instead of sweet fairy music, there rose from the palace such a noise – rattling and shaking, and banging and rustling.

'Whatever can be the matter?' asked Twinkle, Sparkle and Gleam, the moment they arrived.

'We've lost the Wand Star,' sobbed a worried Pixie.

'How dreadful!' gasped Gleam. 'Why, the Wand Star is the most magical thing in the world.'

'Yes,' agreed Sparkle, 'without the star the Queen can work no magic spells.

There'll be no fairy music, no proper fairy stories . . .'

'And no lovely Birthday Ball,' sighed Twinkle, who loved to dance.

'We have searched everywhere,' wept the Pixie. 'The animals have looked too, and so have the fish in the lake. Even the birds helped, before they went to bed – except the Daw family, of course.'

'Why didn't they help?' asked the fairies.

'They were sulking,' the Pixie said crossly. 'I had to chase Papa Daw away from the tree near the Queen's window this morning, because he was giving her a headache. He kept shouting "Jack, Jack" at the kitchen boy. Jack feeds him you see.'

'Well, now,' chuckled Twinkle. 'That gives me an idea.'

She flew off and Sparkle and Gleam sped after her. At last they came to a field where seven tall trees stood. Each tree held several big, untidy nests among its branches.

Twinkle flew straight to the biggest, highest nest of all.

'Mr Daw,' she called softly, and up popped a shiny, black head with bright, beady eyes. He looked very surprised to see a dainty fairy peeping at him.

'Mr Daw,' pleaded Twinkle anxiously. 'You are the head of the Daw family and very clever. Can you get back the Fairy Queen's Wand Star?'

'I *could*,' said Mr Daw huffily, 'but the fairies have been so cross today, I don't see why I *should*. All my family like pretty things, so I expect someone has the star in his nest.'

'The fairies didn't mean to be cross,' coaxed Twinkle. 'And I suppose they shouldn't mind you calling to your friend, Jack, if you didn't call so *loudly*.'

'Well, all right,' cawed Mr Daw more cheerily. 'Let's go and see.' They flew from nest to nest and in the last nest of all, belonging to a very young cousin of Mr Daw, they found the star. The little bird looked so sad at parting with it, that Twinkle felt sorry for him.

'Here,' she smiled, 'there are enough of these jewels for everyone to have one

in his nest.' And she pulled some of the bright stones from her party dress.

Then she flew with her friends straight back to the palace and placed the star on the Fairy Queen's wand.

The Fairy Queen forgave the mischievous Daws, and told them they could have the name Jack for their very own, since they liked it so much. Now they are called the Jackdaw family.

A Present for Amanda

It was Amanda's birthday – she was five years old.

'Happy birthday, dear,' called Mummy and Daddy. 'The postman is here.'

Amanda hurried downstairs feeling very excited.

The postman had brought two parcels – a game from Granny and a sewing set from Aunt Jane – as well as lots of birthday cards from her friends.

But there was no sign of a present from Mummy and Daddy. Surely they had one to give her.

Amanda bit her lip and sat down to breakfast. Afterwards, Mummy said that there was someone waiting to say hello to her in the next room. It was all very mysterious. Amanda ran into the room, but there was nothing unusual in there.

Then a strange, squeaky little voice said, 'Hello! Happy birthday.' She opened her eyes wide in surprise.

'Whatever is it?' asked Amanda.

Daddy chuckled and took a birdcage from under a cover on the sideboard. Inside was a little blue budgerigar.

'He can talk!' cried Amanda.

'Yes, dear,' laughed Mummy, 'and if you're very kind to him, he will learn to say lots of things. His name is Bimbo.'

'Hello, Bimbo,' Amanda said gently.

Bimbo cocked his head on one side. 'Hello,' he squeaked.

'Oh,' cried Amanda, 'what a lovely birthday present! Thank you!'

Look for the next story about Bimbo the budgerigar on page 60.

Mr Bun's Birthday Button

Mr Bun, the white rabbit, had a lovely red jacket. It usually had two bright blue buttons on it but, on the morning of Mr Bun's birthday, it only had one button! Mr Bun had lost one of them while he was out for an early walk in the wood, and he was very upset! He searched for the button everywhere, but he could not find it.

'Oh dear!' he sighed. 'It isn't going to be a very happy birthday.'

Just then, Mr Hurry, the hare, arrived with a big, juicy carrot for Mr Bun's birthday present.

'Many happy returns of the day, and I hope you enjoy this carrot,' he said.

Mr Bun was still feeling rather sad about his lost button, but he tried hard to look happy as he thanked Mr Hurry for the carrot.

Mr Hurry hurried away and, soon after, Mr Muddles, the squirrel arrived.

'Happy birthday, Mr Bun,' said Mr Muddles. 'I'm always forgetting things, I'm afraid, and I forgot it was your birthday today, until Mr Hurry reminded me when I met him in the wood just now. I happened to find this blue button in the wood this morning. It's so big and bright that I thought it would make a lovely birthday present for you.

Mr Bun looked at the button and beamed with delight.

'Mr Muddles,' he said, 'thank you. It's the nicest present you could have brought me. You see, it's the very button I lost from my best red jacket. Fancy you finding it! If I stitch it on straight away, I shall be able to wear the jacket after all. And, as it's my birthday, I'll wear it all day long!'

The Gentle Giant

Tom's Dad had a farm. On it he had tractors, milking-machines, a combine-harvester and other machines to do all the work. But he also had a horse. Tom's Dad loved horses. So he kept Prince, to go to shows, parades and fêtes. Prince used to draw a cart, in which the children had rides, for five pence each. It was great fun riding in the big, old cart.

Prince was a huge horse. He was nearly twice as tall as Tom. Tom had to stoop only a little to walk under Prince's stomach. Even Dad had to reach as high as he could to touch Prince's ears. When Prince went to the blacksmith, to have new shoes put on his hooves, the black-smith would say, 'What a giant of a horse he is! His feet are like frying-pans!'

But Prince was a gentle giant. He would never hurt anyone. When he went on parade, wearing all his shining harness, he allowed Tom to lead him with just one thin rope. Tom walked on ahead, holding the rope, and Prince followed him.

The children cried, 'Oh, look at the little boy leading that giant horse!'

One day, Prince was pulling a cart across a grass-field. Dad was driving, and

Tom was sitting by his side. Suddenly, Prince stopped. It was so sudden that Tom nearly fell out.

'Hey,' shouted Dad. 'What's the matter? Gee up, Prince!'

But Prince stayed quite still, with one of his great front hooves lifted in the air.

'He's afraid to put his foot down,' said Tom.

'So he is,' agreed Dad. 'Perhaps he can see some broken glass. He's a clever horse. I'll jump down and see.'

So Dad jumped down and went to look at the place where Prince was afraid to tread. Then he came back and lifted Tom out of the cart.

'Come quietly,' he whispered. 'Come and see.'

Tom took his father's hand and walked to where Prince's front hoof was still lifted in the air. Down in the grass, just where that great hoof would have landed, was a bright-eyed partridge. She was sitting on a cosy little nest. She looked at them but did not fly away.

'Her eggs must be nearly ready for hatching,' said Dad. 'That's why she won't fly.'

'And Prince must have seen her!' exclaimed Tom.

'Yes,' replied Dad. 'Now there's a clever horse for you. Well done, Prince!'

Then they guided Prince back carefully, and left the partridge to hatch her eggs in the grass.

King of the Toys

Lion was very proud and he would not allow any of the other toys to share his top shelf.

'I am King of the Toys,' he said. 'I am bigger and stronger than anyone.'

One of the little dolls replied, 'The animals in the park are bigger and fiercer than you.'

'Nonsense!' roared Lion, 'I will show them who is King.'

That afternoon when Ann took her doll for a walk in the park, Lion jumped on to the pram and went with them.

At first he loved riding in the pram, but after a while the cats and dogs in the park jumped up at him and he was very frightened. He clung to the doll and was glad when they reached home again.

How the toy animals laughed!

Lion hated being laughed at and felt very sad. Ever since that day in the park he has been the gentlest and kindest toy. Now he shares his top shelf with the other toys, and enjoys their company.

A Tasty Tug of War

Mr Lamb, the butcher had just finished making a long string of delicious meaty sausages. He was hanging them up in his shop window when Bill the Boxer dog walked by.

The sight of those plump, pink sausages dangling in front of his nose was too much of a temptation, even for a well-bred fellow such as Bill. With remarkable speed, he poked his head round the shop door and grabbed the nearest sausage. Then he made off down the street, with a string of at least forty sausages bouncing along behind him.

Bill was making good progress until he reached the end of the street, where there was a roundabout with a statue of a famous gentleman in the middle. On one side of the statue stood a policeman, directing traffic. On the other side, there was Dot the Dalmatian with his two friends, the Terrier pups.

Which way now?

Bill decided that the policeman would be less trouble than Dot and his friends, so he dashed past the busy constable and was half-way round the statue of the famous gentleman, when he met Dot and the Terrier pups coming the other way! They had spotted Bill and his meaty treasure and were determined to have their share.

Bill skidded to a halt, turned round and began to run the other way, with Dot and the Terriers close behind.

On they ran, down one street and up another until they chanced to pass a pet's parlour. There, lots of rather grand dogs were being clipped and shampooed and brushed and fussed over by attendants in white coats.

The dogs had been sitting in the window of the parlour feeling rather bored when Bill and his followers flew past. Well, if there's one thing to liven up a dull morning at a pet's parlour, it's a good chase.

To the alarmed cries of their attendants, half-clipped poodles, soapy sheepdogs and beautifully brushed collies went tearing out of the parlour to join in the fun.

Not far away Bill, who was by this time running out of breath, had reached some fields and a river. With one last burst of speed he plunged into the muddy water and swam to the other side.

Dot and the Terrier pups plunged into the river, too, and when they were all on the other side, Bill decided to make a bargain with them.

'I'll share the sausages with you,' he said, 'if you will help me pull them over to this side of the river before those parlour pets get here.'

So Bill, Dot and the Terrier pups tugged at the sausages, but just as the last one was about to slip into the water on the other side, one soapy sheepdog came bounding up and grabbed it.

Soon the other parlour pets joined in and there was a grand tug of war! Those poor sausages were stretched first one way and then the other across the river. Bill was beginning to think that the battle was never going to end, when a fish popped its head out of the water and bit one of the sausages right in half!

SPLASH! the parlour pets fell into the river head first, while Bill and his team tumbled over backwards, with sausages falling like rain on top of them.

Just then the parlour attendants came running up to catch their runaway customers and took them away at once.

That left just Bill and his friends with a huge pile of sausages all to themselves. So they sat down and ate till there wasn't one sausage left.

25

The Smoke that Thunders

Happy was a baby hippopotamus who lived in the great Zambesi river, in Africa.

In the middle of it were rocks, sticking up just above the surface of the water. Happy and the other hippos liked to bask there in the sunshine. Then, when they became too hot, they rolled off the rocks into the river and sank slowly out of sight under the water.

People in boats often came across the great Zambesi river. They leaned over the side of the boats and watched Happy and the other hippos.

'Do they come especially to see us?' Happy asked his mother.

'No, my dear. They like to watch us, but what they really come to see is *The Smoke That Thunders*,' his mother told him.

Happy was used to living near *The Smoke That Thunders*. Ever since he could remember he had been able to hear the 'thunder'. And whenever he looked eastwards, towards the rising sun, he could see the 'smoke'. As he grew up, he longed to be able to go nearer, to see what it was that made all the noise and the smoke. But his mother said, 'No, Happy. You must never go near it. It is a very dangerous place.'

One day Happy slipped off the rocks and went floating away in the warm river. It was so hot and comfortable, and he was so lazy, that soon he dropped off to sleep. He did not hear his mother and the other hippos shouting to him.

The 'thunder' became louder and louder until it was worse than a hundred lions roaring. Happy found himself being carried along quite fast by the water.

Faster and faster he went, and then, suddenly, his feet touched a rock. He struggled and managed to pull himself out of the water. It was a big flat rock, drenched with water. He walked to the end of it and found himself looking down at . . . NOTHING!

The water suddenly vanished over the edge of a great cliff. It fell down, down, into the dark depths below. Somewhere down there it hit some more rocks, and the spray rose in a mist that was like smoke, and its noise was like thunder. Although he did not know it, Happy was perched on the very edge of one of the biggest waterfalls in the world. They are the Victoria Falls, or, as the Africans call them, *The Smoke That Thunders*.

Poor Happy was very frightened. He couldn't swim back; he couldn't go forward; and, although there were more rocks all along the edge of the waterfall, it looked very dangerous that way.

There are always people at the Victoria Falls, looking at the tumbling water. Soon one of them caught sight of Happy.

'Oh look!' cried a lady. 'There's a baby hippo, stranded on a rock.'

'We must rescue him,' said everyone.

So they brought very strong ropes and iron bars. Then they started to walk, very carefully, across the rocks which were like stepping-stones. They knocked the iron bars into the rocks, to support the rope. And the men tied themselves together, so that none of them could be swept away.

Soon they were near enough to the shivering Happy. One of them threw a lasso that landed round Happy's neck. Then they started to pull.

'Come on,' they shouted. 'Swim!'

Happy seemed to understand and struggled through the water to the next rock. And so the men guided him, with the rope, to the bank of the river.

'Hurrah,' everyone shouted. And they made a little pen for Happy, and gave him some grass and cabbages to eat.

'Perhaps in the morning,' they said, 'we will give him to a zoo.'

But in the night Happy's mother and the other hippos came and pushed against the pen until the sides gave way. So Happy escaped and walked away with them, back to the river.

Perhaps it was just as well, for, although Happy might have enjoyed living in a zoo, he liked living in the great Zambesi river even better. Never again, though, did he go anywhere near *The Smoke That Thunders*.

Teddy Runs Away

Teddy was one of Susan's oldest toys. He had been her favourite for so long that a lot of his fur had worn off where she cuddled him.

But today was Susan's birthday, and her presents were a pretty doll and a fine shiny doll's pram. She was delighted, and after thanking her Mummy and Daddy, she put the doll in the pram and tucked the blue silk cover round her. Then she picked Teddy up and sat him in the other end of the pram. Teddy was pleased – he felt very proud to be going for a ride in the grand new pram.

'May I wheel my pram down the road and show it to Celia?' Susan asked Mummy. Celia was her friend who lived a few houses away.

'If you're very careful and keep on the pavement,' Mummy said. So Susan set off, wheeling her shiny new pram and looking proudly at her doll.

'It's lovely,' said Celia, when she came out and saw the pram. 'You are *lucky*, Susan. And what a pretty doll!' Then she caught sight of Teddy, looking rather battered but very pleased with himself.

'Fancy putting that old Teddy in!' cried Celia. 'He's so old and funny-looking. I wouldn't put him in my new pram, if I had one!'

Celia promised to come and play later, and Susan wheeled her pram home again. When she got home she took Teddy out of the pram and put him on a chair.

'I shan't take you out in the pram any more,' she said. 'You're such an old Teddy now!'

Then she heard Celia knocking, and ran out to play with her and the new doll and pram.

Teddy felt very sad. 'I won't stay here now that Susan likes the doll better than me,' he thought. 'I'll go out in the world and seek my fortune!'

While Susan and Celia were busy playing with the pram, Teddy crept out and started down the garden path. After a long time he came to a wall at the end of the garden. It seemed so high to him that while he was sitting thinking how to climb it, he fell fast asleep!

Susan had a lovely birthday. Several of her friends came to tea, and Mummy had made her a cake with candles on top. When the day was over, and Susan was tucked up in bed, she realised that something was missing!

'Where's Teddy?' said Susan. 'I can't go to sleep without him.'

Mummy suggested taking the new doll to bed instead, but Susan said the

fire. Then she took him upstairs to Susan and sat him on her bed.

'You had left him right down the end of the garden,' Mummy said. 'I suppose it was when you and Celia were playing with the pram.

Susan did not like to say that she had taken Teddy out because Celia thought he was too old and shabby for the new pram. Anyway, Teddy was back, and he was dry by now, so she hugged him and curled up to go to sleep.

As for Teddy, he decided to forget all about the new doll and seeking his fortune. He was very glad to be back with Susan after his adventure.

doll was too knobbly to cuddle and she wanted Teddy.

Mummy looked for him in every room of the house. Finally, she went out into the garden, and found Teddy right down the end, by the wall. It was beginning to get dark and his fur was damp with dew.

'There you are!' said Mummy, and she took him in and dried him by the

Miss Smith's Black Cat

Miss Smith's black cat, Tibs, would drink nothing but orange juice. No matter how hard Miss Smith tried to make him drink milk, he refused.

'I don't know what to do,' said Miss Smith to Sam the fishmonger's boy. 'If Tibs doesn't drink milk, he will be ill.'

Sam thought she was making a lot of fuss about nothing, but he liked Miss Smith so he said he would see what he could do. He found Tibs sitting on a log cleaning his whiskers.

'Hello,' said Sam, cheerfully.

'Miaow,' answered Tibs. 'Have you brought my fish?'

'Of course,' said Sam. He sat on the log beside Tibs. 'Did you know Miss Smith is worried about you?' he asked.

'Me! Miaow! Why?' asked Tibs in surprise.

'She thinks you will be ill if you don't drink milk,' said Sam.

'Of course I won't,' miaowed Tibs. 'I don't like milk.'

'Well, that won't stop Miss Smith worrying,' said Sam. He thought for a moment. 'Will you drink just half a saucer of milk a day to make her happy?' he asked.

'I could manage that,' said Tibs. He liked Miss Smith, too. She was very good to him.

'Good,' said Sam. 'And because you will be drinking something you don't really like to please Miss Smith, I shall bring you an extra piece of fish every Tuesday.'

Tibs was delighted and thought that he would gladly put up with the milk in return for that extra piece of fish!

Hungry Hedgehog

Little Fat Hedgehog pushed his way through a pile of autumn leaves in search of food. He was hungry, and it was cold, so he was hoping to find some grubs or insects so that he could have a nice big meal before his winter sleep. He ambled slowly across the dark garden, with grass and dry leaves sticking to his prickles. He was just sniffing around cautiously when, to his surprise, he saw four bright green lights gleaming brightly at the end of the garden. Poor Little Fat Hedgehog stood quite still, terrified, as two large black cats came stalking up to him, tails waving.

'Hello, you funny creature,' said the first one. 'Why are you so sharp and spiney?'

'Why are your legs so short?' asked the second cat, rudely.

But by then, Little Fat Hedgehog had curled up quickly into a tight, round ball, with his prickles out and his face hidden right away inside. He stayed very still as the cats came nearer.

'You pat and I'll poke', said the first one, and they prodded Little Fat Hedgehog. But what a shock they had . . .

'My nose!' shrieked one, feeling the sharp spines.

'My paw!' squealed the other. Tails streaming behind, they both fled down the garden and away over the fence. Little Fat Hedgehog chuckled and slowly uncurled. Then he saw that the cats had knocked over their bowl of milk in their hurry to escape. The milk was trickling slowly towards him in a white stream. 'That looks good!' thought Little Fat Hedgehog, and he drank every drop.

The sky grew lighter as morning came. An owl flew high overhead, calling softly as it flew back to its tall tree in the distant woods.

'I don't want him to catch me for his breakfast,' said Little Fat Hedgehog, trotting towards a pile of golden leaves in the corner of the garden by the shed. He was feeling sleepy, so he shuffled into the leaves and settled down. All around, it was still and quiet, apart from the gentle sounds of waking birds. Soon he was fast asleep, with the dry leaves blowing lightly over him.

Little Fat Hedgehog slept there all through the cold winter, tucked in his cosy, leafy bed behind the garden shed, until the warm spring days came to wake him up again.

A Sad Day for Leonard the Lion

The day the King flew into the statue of his Great Aunt Caroline, was a very sad day indeed. It was sad for the King because he had ruined his new aeroplane but it was even sadder for Leonard the lion because he was now out of a job.

Leonard was a statue, too. For years he had sat at the foot of Great Aunt Caroline's column, as a sort of body guard. He had looked very proud and business-like, as one should look in such an important position.

However, unlike any other statue in the world, Leonard had feelings. And, right now, Leonard was feeling very fed up.

What was to become of him? He couldn't guard a statue that wasn't there.

Leonard soon discovered that the King had no intention of replacing his Great Aunt. He hadn't much cared for the statue and anyway, it got in the way of his flying which was all he really cared about.

'Clear it all away!' the King ordered his soldiers, pointing to a pile of rubble that had once been Great Aunt Caroline. When they came to move Leonard, one soldier asked the King, 'What shall we do with the lion, sir . . . now that he has nothing to guard.'

'Nothing to guard! Nothing to guard!' shouted the King. 'There must be something he can do. Now, let me see. I know, he can guard the lilies on my pond and stop those wretched pelicans from pecking the petals.'

So poor Leonard was lifted by a crane on to a lorry and driven round to the lily pond. He felt it was most undignified for an important lion like him to be sitting in the back of a lorry.

Well, I ask you. Have you ever heard of a lion in charge of a lily pond! It made poor Leonard feel so silly, and the pelicans took no notice of him at all.

One morning, the King was reading his newspaper by the lily pond. He was looking at the advertisements to see if there were any second-hand aeroplanes for sale, since he couldn't afford to buy a new one. Suddenly he spotted an advertisement that read:

'Wanted. Statue of important-looking lion for stately home. Good price paid. Please notify the Duchess.'

Well, its surprising what you will find in newspapers, but there it was.

The King looked at Leonard. Leonard put on his most important-looking expression and stared back at the King.

'That's it,' cried the King. 'I'll sell Leonard to the Duchess, then he will have a proper job again and I shall have enough money to buy a new aeroplane!'

So it was settled. The King's soldiers put Leonard on to the lorry again and took him to the stately home. There he was lifted into place on one side of the Main Gates. On the other side sat a splendid-looking unicorn. What a fine pair they made!

Leonard was very happy now and the Duchess thought that he was the most handsome lion she had ever seen. And all the visitors who passed through the Main Gates to the stately home thought so too.

Sometimes, the King would fly over in his new aeroplane and wave to Leonard, just to make sure that he was enjoying his new life with the Duchess.

Two Friends

Two friends were walking through the woods when a bear sprang out upon them. One of the friends ran away, climbed a tree and hid himself, while the other stayed on the path.

What could he do? Only fall on his face and make believe he was dead.

The bear came right up and sniffed him, and he held his breath.

Smelling his face, the bear thought he was dead and went away.

When the bear was gone, the boy in the tree climbed down, laughing.

'Tell me,' he said, 'what did that bear whisper in your ear?'

'Oh, he told me never to trust people who run from their friends when they are in great danger.'

Road Drill for the Hedgehogs

The autumn leaves were drifting down, and Bumble and Tailymouse crouched in the warm mousehole under the oak tree.

Suddenly, a small, gruff voice called down the hole, 'Are you there? Can you come up for a moment?'

Bumble and Tailymouse climbed up the passage to see who had called.

'Well! It is Prickle and Spikey!' said Bumble. 'You were such tiny hedgehogs last time I saw you!'

'We have a *problem*,' said Prickle, 'and it is very urgent. Mother Hedgehog has gone to live in the big wood across the main road, and we want to join her. But you see, Bumble, when we hear a car coming, we are so frightened that we curl up into a ball and we never manage to get across the road.'

'Now, let's think,' said kind old Bumble. 'You need some sort of training. I *know*! Go down to the Nursery School in the morning, creep under the window and listen to the teacher giving the children their Road Drill. You are *bound* to learn what to do.'

'Oh, thank you Bumble,' said Prickle. 'You are clever!'

The following morning, the two little hedgehogs hurried down the lane, and through the gate which led to the school-room window.

'You stand on my back,' said Spikey, 'and you may be able to hear what they are saying.'

'Attention, children, please!' said the teacher. 'Now we are going to start by saying our Road Drill before we have lessons. All together now . . . One, two, three . . . *Look to the right, look to the left, look to the right again, and if the road is clear go quickly across.* Good! Now I am going to give a prize to the boy or girl who can make up the best verse on our drill, and give it to me tomorrow!'

Prickle jumped down and took Spikey's paw. 'Come on!' he said, 'We must go. I know just what to do now.'

Bumble and Tailymouse were just coming home for supper, when they saw the two little hedgehogs standing on the edge of the big main road. The cars were racing by. Prickle and Spikey waited patiently side by side.

Then Bumble heard their little voices, 'One, two, three . . . Look to the right, look to the left . . .'

Bumble closed her eyes and gave a silent prayer for their safety. When she opened them again, she could see two prickly little forms hurrying through the wood on the other side of the road. They were safe!

Next day, when the teacher came into the classroom, the children were waiting with their entries for the competition. Suddenly a large leaf floated in through the window, and landed on her desk. On it, in thin, shaky writing, was scrawled:

> 'If you look to the right,
> And there's nothing in sight,
> Then you look to the left, my dear.
> Look back to the right,
> Still nothing in sight,
> Go quickly across, if it's clear.'

'*Who* sent this?' said the teacher. 'Why, its a wonderful verse, and worth a prize!'

But nobody had any idea, and only Prickle and Spikey, safe with their mother in the big wood, knew about Robin who had offered to take their verse to the school.

Balloons in the Market Square

'What's today?' wondered Rosie as she lay dreamily beneath the snug bedclothes in her little attic room. 'I know! It's market day and there will be lots of animals down in the square. The balloon man will be there too!'

She jumped out of bed and threw on her clothes. Then she went helter-skelter down the stairs, gobbled her breakfast and ran outside. Good Dog followed her – he liked to go everywhere with Rosie.

Rosie's friends, Meg and Sally and Jenny and Sam, were waiting outside her house, and they all skipped across the road to the square.

'We're going to look at all the animals, balloon man,' chorused the children. 'Do you want to come too?'

'I'd love to,' said the balloon man. And he gave each of them a lovely bright balloon to carry.

They visited the billy-goat first. While Rosie was telling Good Dog to sit quietly, the billy-goat chewed through the string on her orange balloon.

'Oh!' she cried, watching it float away.

Sam ran on to see the big bull, who glared at him and butted the fence with his horns.

'Bang!' went the yellow balloon.

'Oh no!' wailed Sam.

Meg was leaning over the fence chatting to the sheep next door. Suddenly, she dropped her striped balloon.

'Pop!' went the balloon beneath the sheep's hooves.

Meanwhile, Jenny had found some ponies to talk to. They nibbled curiously at her spotted balloon.

'Bang!' Jenny's balloon had burst too.

Sally was watching the chickens over the fence. Suddenly, they all ran up and pecked at her balloon.

'Pop!' went the balloon.

'Oh dear!' sighed Sally.

The old balloon man smiled as the children came up with sad faces.

'Cheer up,' he said. 'I have five balloons left – that's just enough to go round.'

'Thank you balloon man,' they cried, and they all ran off to play with their new balloons, well away from the animals.

Old Jason's Faithful Sheepdog

Far out on the hills, Old Jason the shepherd was up early with his sheep, leading them over the moors to find grassy places where they could feed. The spring weather was chilly and he walked briskly, with Sally the sheepdog bounding at his side.

'Come on, Sally,' he said to the dog. 'Keep those sheep together for me – we don't want them straying too far away while they feed.'

The sheepdog was clever. She always knew exactly what Old Jason wanted her to do and she understood every word, whistle or sign that he made. She chased here and there, barking at the sheep and keeping them together. The sheep ran everywhere and Old Jason often laughed at them.

'Silly old sheep, aren't they!' he said to Sally, watching them run up and down the green hillside. They bleated and wagged their tails, the young lambs pushing to keep up with their mothers.

At dinner time, Old Jason ate sandwiches and drank a mug of hot tea. Sally shared the tea but she didn't take her eyes off the sheep. She knew that they could stray a long way over the wild moors.

By evening, Old Jason was tired and as the sun began to go down he counted the sheep and lambs to make sure they were all there.

'Right, Sally, we've got them all,' he said to the sheepdog as she raced down the hill, but Sally wanted to tell him something. She jumped up at Old Jason, barking loudly. She tugged at him then ran up the hill.

Old Jason followed. Right at the top of the hill was one of the lambs, bleating loudly. It wasn't hurt but its foot was caught between two boulders and its woolly coat was tangled up in a prickly thorn bush.

'I must have counted wrongly,' said Old Jason. 'What a good thing I have a sheepdog to help me.' He carefully released the lamb and then he patted Sally. 'You're a good dog,' he said as she chased

the lamb down the hill to its mother. You know those sheep as well as I do. I *am* lucky to have such a faithful dog.'

Then they went home together through the spring evening – the sheep jostling, the lambs skipping, the dog running here and there and the old shepherd humming softly to himself, looking forward to his supper.

Prince to the Rescue

One evening Peter and his father went for a walk by the river. They took Prince, their big alsatian dog, with them.

Prince loved those walks! He would bound ahead, wait until they caught up with him, and then off he would go again.

But this evening, to their surprise, Prince suddenly jumped from the bank into the river.

Peter and his father saw him swimming towards something small and dark that was struggling in the water.

Peter jumped with excitement. 'What do you think Prince has found?' he cried.

'We shall know in a minute,' his father answered, as they watched the big dog returning with something in his mouth.

When Prince reached the bank he proudly laid a tiny black kitten at Peter's feet.

'Good dog!' Peter cried. 'You have saved the little kitten's life!'

Prince licked the kitten gently and then looked first at Peter and then at his father, as if to say, 'It belongs to us now. We must take care of it.'

They wrapped the little animal in Peter's scarf and took it home. Peter's Mummy gave it some warm milk and laid it on a rug in front of the fire. Daddy pinned a note to the gate asking if anyone had lost a kitten, but no-one ever called to claim it.

Prince, who loved mothering animals, would lie down quite close to the kitten to make sure no harm would come to it.

Very soon they were the greatest of friends, and the little kitten always went with Prince when Peter and Daddy took him for his evening walk.

The Golden Web

Dick and his mother lived in a cottage by a wood. They were very poor and made a living by selling firewood in the next town.

One day, when he was chopping wood, Dick saw a spider. It had fallen on to a tree trunk and its legs were caught on the sticky sap. However hard it tried, the spider could not free itself.

Being a kind-hearted boy, Dick carefully unstuck each leg and put the spider on to a leaf. Imagine his surprise when the spider spoke to him!

'Since you freed me from the tree,' it said, 'I should like to do you a good turn. Take me home with you and I shall repay your kindness.'

Dick did as the spider asked. 'Mother, Mother,' he called as he ran into the cottage, 'see what I have found.'

His mother came out from the kitchen.

'Why, it's only an old spider,' she said. 'Throw it away. We don't want spiders in the house.'

Dick told his mother what had happened in the wood.

'Very well,' she said, 'it can stay for one night, but after that, out it goes. And that is final!'

In the morning, Dick and his mother found hanging in front of the fireplace the most beautiful web they had ever seen. It was made of gold and shone out from the dark corner like a sunbeam.

They thanked the spider and took the web to town in order to sell it.

The shopkeeper who bought it was astonished to see the web. He paid a lot of money for it and Dick bought food and clothes for his mother and himself.

Every day Dick found another golden web. He and his mother repainted the cottage and bought animals for the

Dick and his mother were out, they crept into the house and grabbed the spider. They put it into a small, wooden box and ran off.

The next morning, the men eagerly opened the wooden box expecting to see a golden web inside. When all they saw was a spider, they were cross.

'Why haven't you spun us a web?' they cried. 'You nasty horrid thing!' And they shook the box.

The spider crawled out of the box before they could shut the lid and ran across the floor, up the wall and through the window before they could catch him.

When it reached the street, the spider saw a donkey pulling a cart full of grain. Quickly, it crawled under one of the sacks and stayed there until the cart passed Dick's cottage. Then it scuttled up the path and back into the house.

Dick and his mother were delighted to see the spider again and all that winter it spun them golden webs. When the spring came, Dick took the spider back to the wood where he had found it and thanked it before he said goodbye.

'You have more than repaid me,' Dick said. 'The farm will keep us in comfort for the rest of our lives.' So he left the spider on a tree.

The spider was happy to be back in the wood again. And who knows, maybe he is still spinning webs of gold.

farm. But the shopkeeper was curious.

'Where does Dick find the golden webs?' he thought, and he hired two men to follow Dick home.

That night, when the men looked through the window, they saw the spider spinning a golden web. They decided not to tell the shopkeeper, but to steal the spider for themselves. When

Glossy Keeps Watch

'Now, Glossy,' called Daddy Starling, 'stand on this branch. If you see anything coming, squawk!'

It was the first time that Glossy, the young starling with the shining head, had kept watch while his mother and father, his aunts and uncles and their friends, Mr and Mrs Sparrow with their two little children, had a meal of crumbs on the garden lawn.

Soon they were joined by Miss Pompous Pigeon, who hated to be left out of anything that was fun.

Just as Mrs Sparrow found a nice soft crumb for Dot and Tiny Sparrow, Glossy saw something brown jumping along the edge of the grass.

'*Squark*, squar, squar, squark, squar, squar,' he cried.

At once all the birds lifted themselves off the ground and hid high up in the trees out of harm's way.

'Flutter my feathers,' said Miss Pompous Pigeon, crossly, 'it's only a piece of brown paper.'

'Never mind, Glossy, old son,' said Daddy Starling. 'A squawk too soon is better than a squawk too late.'

The birds flew back to the crumbs.

Then, not far away and coming nearer, he saw something much bigger than the brown paper.

'Squark, squar, squar,' he cried.

Up into the trees flew Daddy and Mummy Starling and all the others.

'Flutter my feathers,' said Miss Pompous Pigeon, very crossly. 'It's only the little girl from the house, bringing more crumbs and nice fresh water.'

Down to the crumbs flew the birds again, and for a while nothing could be heard but 'Peck-peck-peck'.

Then Glossy saw something black creeping slowly along the edge of the grass. He knew that he must squawk for all he was worth, because it was the *big black cat*.

'Squark,' Glossy cried out. 'Squark, squark!'

'Not again!' cawed Miss Pompous Pigeon. 'Well, I'm not moving.'

So she stayed, pecking the crumbs, but all the other birds flew into the trees out of the cat's way.

'S-q-u-a-r-k!' Glossy cried. And this time he fell off the branch and landed right beside Miss Pompous Pigeon. She was so surprised, she flew to the very top of the tree.

'Splendid, old son,' shouted Daddy Starling. 'You have even frightened the big black cat away!'

And all the birds laughed and laughed.

There is another exciting story about Glossy the starling on page 98.

Dabby's First Quack

Little Dabby Duckling could not say *quack*! She tried and she tried, but all she could manage was a funny little cheep.

'Don't worry,' Mother Duck told her. 'You'll say it one day – one day when you're not even thinking about it.'

Dabby tried not to worry, but she knew that all the other folk on Sunny Dale Farm would laugh at her if she did not manage to say *quack* soon.

Dabby sat at the edge of the pond, feeling very sorry for herself, when along came Roger, the farmer's small son.

'Look at my lovely balloons, Dabby,' said Roger.

He had been given two – a yellow one and a green one. Roger was pleased with his balloons, and he ran round and round the pond, with the balloons bobbing along behind him on their strings. But he wasn't holding the strings tightly enough, and suddenly, the yellow balloon drifted away. The breeze carried it towards a holly bush nearby. The balloon brushed against one of the prickly leaves, and suddenly . . . *bang* . . . the balloon burst! The noise was so loud that Dabby, who had been sitting near the holly bush, tumbled into the pond, with a loud *quack*! She had said *quack* without even trying!

Roger was not too sad about his balloon, for he still had another one. As for Dabby, she was delighted that she had managed to say *quack* at last. Mother Duck was pleased too.

Dabby walked round the farmyard, quacking proudly. If ever you should go by Sunny Dale Farm, you're sure to hear her!

What Colour
are Elephants?

Before his father and mother took him to live in East Africa, Keith had only seen elephants at the zoo.

'When we go into the game parks in East Africa,' his father told him, 'you will see wild elephants, and lions and zebras and giraffes, and lots of other animals. They'll all be there for us to see in their natural state.'

Keith looked forward to seeing them all, especially the elephants. He was fascinated by elephants.

After they had arrived in East Africa, Keith's father took Keith and his mother in a Land Rover to look for elephants. The game park was an enormous place, reaching as far as Keith could see in every direction. It was grassy country, but the grass had been burned brown by the hot sun. The soil beneath was red – the colour of bricks. Dotted about over the plain were groups of trees. Most of them

were trees with flat tops and lots of thorns. And under the trees there were high mounds of red earth, like giant sand-castles. Some of them were taller than the Land Rover and even as tall as the trees.

'Those are ant-hills,' said Keith's father.

'Ant-hills!' exclaimed Keith. 'Are they big ants?'

'No,' said his father. 'Just ordinary-sized ones. It takes them a long time to build these giant hills.'

The Land Rover jolted along for a long time. Keith and his father and mother saw zebras, ostriches, antelopes and a rhinoceros, but they could not find an elephant.

They stopped for a moment, so that Keith's Dad could look at his map.

'That's an extra big ant-hill,' said Keith, pointing to some trees just ahead. Then he gasped.

'Oh, look! It's moving!'

So it was. It moved out from under the shadow of the trees, stretched itself and flapped its big ears. It was an elephant! And, as they watched, four or five other 'ant-hills' turned into elephants!

'Well, fancy that!' exclaimed Keith's mother. 'They were there all the time. Perhaps we've seen other elephants without knowing it.'

'But – but, they're red!' said Keith.

'That's because they've been rubbing themselves against the ant-hills,' his father explained. 'They're covered with red soil. They enjoy a dust-bath.'

Keith watched them in wonder.

'If my teacher ever asks me what colour elephants are,' he said, 'I shall tell her they're red. And I shall say I know because I've seen them.'

'But I don't think she'll believe me!' he added, with a grin.

Magellan the Clever Mynah Bird

One fine, sunny day, Annabel went down to the pet shop with her mother and father and Leonard the labrador.

'Annabel and Leonard would like a new friend,' said Father to the man behind the counter.

'I have just the thing,' smiled the pet shop man. 'It's a strange little creature that can talk to all the animals. It's called a mynah bird.'

They all went over to the corner, and there, between some puppies and a pair of rabbits, sat a wonderful bird.

'My name is Magellan,' it said in a voice that was almost the same as Father's.

Annabel was very surprised! 'But, can you talk to Leonard, too?' asked Annabel, eagerly.

'Woof, woof. Of course I can,' replied Magellan smugly. Leonard pricked up his ears and looked pleased.

'He's exactly the pet for us,' said Mother, and they went off together all talking at once.

The Day the Cuckoo Left his Clock

In Mary's house there was a cuckoo clock on the wall. Every time the clock struck the hour, a cuckoo came out from behind two small doors.

Everybody depended on the cuckoo. Mary's Daddy always set his watch by it. He waited for it to call *cuckoo* eight times before catching his bus for work each morning, during the week.

As everyone loved the clock, they would have been very surprised if they could have heard the cuckoo talking to himself angrily one morning.

'What use am I?' he said, 'I'm stuck here in this silly old clock. Last time I looked out I saw other birds enjoying themselves in the garden, and I have to stay here by myself.'

The cuckoo became crosser and crosser each day. Every time he finished calling *cuckoo*, he would slam the door crossly. 'That's enough!' he would mutter angrily.

One day, he saw snow in the garden. It was very deep.

'What lovely white stuff,' he thought. 'What fun it would be to jump up and down in it! Why am I always stuck here missing all the fun?'

Just then his spring broke. He shot right out of the clock and through the window, which had been left open.

'I'm flying at last,' he said happily, as he shot gaily through the air.

Then he landed with a thump in the snow outside. What a shock he had! Snow was not a bit as he had imagined.

'Oh, it's all nasty and wet. You can't jump up and down in it at all. How cold it is out here.'

As he looked round, some of the birds flew down to him.

'What a strange bird!' said the robin, looking him up and down.

'Go away,' said the blackbird, 'there's not enough food for proper birds like us. We don't want to share it with you.'

All the birds turned away from the cuckoo. The poor cuckoo cried. He could not fly away as he had no wings. Without the clock, he could not move at all. He slowly sank deeper and deeper into the snow. The birds flew away and left him there. He was very lonely and unhappy.

Next morning, Mary's Daddy was late for work. There was no cuckoo in the clock to remind him of the time.

Mary missed the cuckoo. She thought the house sounded very quiet without the little bird.

'Why don't you take your sledge out, Mary?' asked her Mummy. 'There is a lot of snow in the garden now. It should be fun if you put your warm clothes on.'

Mary put on her coat, her warm gloves and boots. She took her sledge into the garden. Mary was just going past the window when she saw something in the snow. It was the little cuckoo.

That night Mary's Daddy fixed a new spring to the cuckoo and put him back in the clock.

The cuckoo was happy to be back in his clock again. He was warm and comfortable once more and proud to know how much he had been missed. And he never wanted to go on an adventure into the world outside again!

The Adventurous Young Rabbit

One bright, sunny morning, Bobtail the rabbit opened his eyes and looked around him in the burrow where he lived with his Mummy, Daddy, his sister Katy, and his two brothers, Billy and Sammy.

It was a lovely morning and the sun shone into the burrow. Bobtail crept out of his little bed very quietly.

'I'm going to have an adventure,' he said to himself. 'Nobody is awake yet, so I'll sneak out.'

He had always wanted to explore the fields beyond, but his parents had forbidden him to go, as he was the youngest of the family, and they were afraid some harm might come to him if he wandered off alone. Very carefully, he crept towards the door, had a last look round at all his family fast asleep, then hopped out into the field.

Bobtail took in a deep breath of fresh air, then he scampered through the field of wheat and saw there were vegetable plots beyond the fence. So he jumped over the bottom bar of the fence and landed in a patch of luscious, fresh lettuces, carrots, onions and radishes.

Bobtail started on the lettuce, and then ate so many carrots he thought he would burst. Soon, he began to feel very tired, so he made himself comfortable among the lettuces and went fast asleep.

Bobtail did not know how long he had been asleep. He was suddenly woken up by a huge dog bending over him and tapping him with his paw. Bobtail jumped up quickly, gave out a loud squeal and was through the fence and away like lightning, with the dog chasing after him. Luckily, the dog soon gave up and went away, barking.

After a few minutes' rest by the side of a road, he was on his feet again. He looked around and saw a wood on the other side of the road.

'Good!' he thought. 'I'll be safe in there.' As he started to run across the road a big car came racing by, just missing Bobtail. The noisy hooter gave him an awful fright.

He reached the edge of the wood and went deeper and deeper into it. Suddenly, he felt something biting him and he let out a yell. A weasel was attacking him. Bobtail fought to be free and ran away as fast as his legs could carry him. By the time he reached the other side of the wood he was breathless. He longed to be at home again, and he decided he would try to find his way back.

Bobtail knew that he would get a scolding from his Daddy for running away, so he scampered back as fast as he could.

Soon he caught sight of his family. They were calling him, and his brothers and sister were chasing across the field looking for him. When they saw Bobtail they shouted with delight, they were so pleased to see him safe and sound. He might have been away for days, the fuss they made of him. His Mummy took him close to her and held him tight.

'My little Bobtail,' she said. 'Thank goodness we've found you.'

He could not help but cry, he was so happy to be home.

'Don't cry now, my boy,' Daddy said. 'But remember – no running away again. You are home and safe now, but another time you might not be so lucky. Now tell us where you have been and all about your adventures, Bobtail.'

So Bobtail sat down on the soft green grass, with his family round him and told them all about his adventures beyond the field.

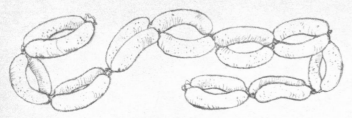

Sam Saves the Sausages

Sam was a dachshund – one of those long, low dogs that people often call sausage dogs!

Jenny and James, who owned Sam, always called him Sausage Dog. They said it fondly, but Sam didn't like it. He grumbled to Paws, the cat.

'Never mind, Sam,' said Paws. 'You are still only a puppy. If you eat a lot, you will soon grow big and strong like me, and you won't be quite so low.'

'Thank you for the advice, Paws,' woofed Sam.

He went into the kitchen to see if his dinner was ready. There was nothing in his bowl but on the table there was a string of sausages for the children's dinner – and standing by the table was a big, brown dog. The big, brown dog had come in through the back door, and was just about to jump up and take the sausages. Sam was a brave fellow and, because he was so long and low, he was able to slip in between the legs of the big dog. The big dog tumbled over Sam, and was so surprised that he picked himself up without a word and hurried out of the kitchen.

'I'm sorry,' he called back to Sam, 'but the sausages smelt so nice.'

'Be off with you! Go home and eat your own dinner!' barked Sam.

Jenny and James heard Sam barking. They ran into the kitchen and saw him standing at the door, watching the big dog running off down the garden path.

'Sam, you saved the sausages!' they cheered. 'You saved our dinner! What a brave Sausage Dog!'

Sam didn't mind being called Sausage Dog now. In fact, he was quite proud of the name Jenny and James had given him.

Patience has a Holiday

Mr Joe was the donkey man at the seaside and every day he led Patience, his donkey, up and down the sands giving rides to the children.

One hot day, Mr Joe decided to take Patience home to his nearby cottage for a rest in the cool garden.

Mrs Joe was in the garden hanging out washing. Joe led Patience through the gate and left her in the garden while he fetched her a drink. Mrs Joe was just pegging a flowery sheet on the line when two grey ears appeared over the top and a nose pushed its way between the sheets. 'Oh my goodness!' shrieked Mrs Joe.

'Hee-haw,' brayed Patience loudly. Mrs Joe was so startled that she dropped the pegs, and the flowery sheet fell off the line and on to the donkey. Patience trampled on it, wound herself up in it, then ran past Joe who was just coming back with a drink.

Before Mr and Mrs Joe could stop her, she pushed her way through to the kitchen door, looked inside and helped herself to some carrots in a basket.

Then she ran back down the garden, getting more and more tangled in the flowery sheet. She squeezed through a hole in the hedge and out into the lane, where she looked all round her, nose and ears poking out through the sheet.

A car drove along and pulled up. A van stopped behind the car and a bicycle drew in beside the van. Then a post van and a farm truck came along behind. They all hooted and tooted loudly at Mr and Mrs Joe, who had caught Patience and were trying to disentangle her from the flowery sheet.

Joe didn't want his donkey to be frightened. He led Patience back into the garden and the traffic moved on.

'Come on Patience, have your drink, then you're going back to the beach. One afternoon's holiday is quite enough for me,' said Joe, mopping his brow.

The children on the beach were pleased to see Patience back again.

'She's had a marvellous time,' said Joe with feeling. 'But she seems quite ready to get back to work! She'll give some more rides when it's cooler. As long as they're treated kindly, donkeys like hard work.'

'It's a good thing I like hard work too,' said Mrs Joe with a smile, as she washed the bright, flowery sheet for the second time that day.

Potter has a Bath

'Potter!' called Mrs Berry, the farmer's wife, looking over the pig-sty. 'Potter Pig, it really is time you had a bath!'

'A bath? Me?' said Potter, looking up from his trough which Mrs Berry had just filled with vegetable scraps.

'Yes, you,' smiled Mrs Berry.

Potter was horrified at the thought of such a thing.

'You are quite the grubbiest little animal in the farmyard,' went on Mrs Berry. 'You cannot imagine how much nicer you would look scrubbed and pink and clean. I can see *I* shall have to do something about it.' And with that Mrs Berry walked away, rattling her vegetable bucket as she went.

'Oh, dear,' thought Potter. 'Mrs Berry means business.' He wanted to please her. She was so kind and always brought him the tastiest scraps from her kitchen. But the idea of Mrs Berry giving him a sweet-smelling, soapy bath was unbearable.

'I think I'll go and ask some friends if there is any other way of keeping clean,' said Potter, in the hope of finding out before Mrs Berry came back.

Potter was just trotting across the yard when he saw a group of sparrows, splashing about in a puddle.

'Ah, just the thing,' said Potter as he stopped to watch the little birds dipping and shaking their feathers in the muddy pool. Potter got as far as plunging his snout in the puddle and blowing a few bubbles to see how cold the water was, when the little birds chattered and chirped at Potter to stop.

'Please stop doing that,' said the smallest sparrow. 'You are far too big for this tiny puddle and, anyway, we were here well before you arrived.'

'Quite so, quite so,' said Potter politely. 'No harm meant,' and he trotted off to see the farm cats.

Mrs Tabby was sitting surrounded by four beautiful kittens in a pile of straw. 'Hello, Potter,' she purred. 'Aren't my little ones just adorable?'

Potter agreed that they did look lovely.

'They keep themselves so clean,' went on Mrs Tabby proudly. Then she began to wash herself, licking her paws and rubbing her face and ears with them, till her fur was smooth and shiny.

Potter blushed a little, and tried to rub a muddy patch on one ear with his trotter, so that Mrs Tabby should not see. However, Potter was wobbling about so much on three legs, that Mrs Tabby did see, all too clearly, and she said kindly, 'No, Potter dear. *You* will never clean your ears like that. What you need is a good *scrub*.'

That very word had Potter running for his life, out into the yard and . . .

whooosh . . . straight into a jet of icy cold water.

Farmer Berry was washing his tractor in the yard with a hose. How poor Potter shivered and squealed, all the way back to his sty!

Mrs Berry came into the yard to see what all the fuss was about.

'Now where's my grubby little pig,' she said peering over the sty. 'Well,' said Mrs Berry, looking at Potter who was looking considerably cleaner from his shower. 'I see you have really tried to clean yourself for me,' and she gave him a little hug. 'Now I won't have to use any soap, but I will just finish you off with some nice warm water and scrub your back with a tickly brush.'

When Potter was nice and pink and warm all over, Mrs Berry gave him a trough full of mash and fresh vegetables.

'There,' said Mrs Berry, 'that wasn't so bad, was it?'

And Potter, who had secretly loved all the fuss Mrs Berry had made of him, agreed that it wasn't bad at all!

A Flying Lesson with Mr Mervin Mole

Mr Mervin Mole lived in a pillar-box because he didn't like getting his hands dirty digging holes like other moles. Being rather clever, he found himself a clean, comfortable home instead.

Bang! Bang! Bang! Someone was knocking on Mervin's door. 'At this time of morning!' he yawned, and decided it might be something important so he had better get up. It was rather late in the morning anyway.

He peeped out of the pillar-box and saw Mr Matthew Mouse and Mr Orlando Owl, standing outside and looking worried.

Mervin climbed down to find out what the trouble was. Orlando was upset because his son, who was already three months old, still could not fly. He asked if Mervin could help.

'I'll try,' said Mervin. He got ready, then helped Matthew into his balloon, which the postman had given him for Christmas. Then they followed Orlando to the wood to find his little son.

It was true. Orlando's son couldn't fly. 'Mm, now then,' said Mervin, pacing thoughtfully up and down. 'Mm, well. Mm, well, well.' And he went on pacing and thinking.

'Got it!' said Mervin, grabbing the little owl by the wing. 'Follow me!' he yelled and led his friends back to his balloon.

'Will it carry all of us?' asked Orlando.

'Of course,' said Mervin, and proceeded to push the little owl into the basket of the balloon.

Mervin pulled out the anchor and climbed aboard. Soon the four friends were floating high above the wood.

'Now then,' said Mervin, and produced a little red balloon from his jacket pocket.

'What's the good of that?' asked Orlando, looking angry. Mervin just laughed and started to blow up the balloon. Soon, it was big and round.

54

To his friends' amazement Mervin tied the string of the balloon around the middle of the astonished little owl.

'Are you quite sure you know what you are doing, Mervin?' asked Orlando, who was really cross now.

'Here we go!' yelled Mervin and pushed the little owl out of the balloon. 'Watch out!' hooted Orlando. 'Don't worry,' shouted Mervin. 'Whoops!' said Matthew.

Orlando need not have worried. The balloon held the little owl up and by flapping his wings he was soon happily flying around the treetops, hooting joyfully at the top of his voice.

Mervin, Orlando and Matthew followed the little owl. 'Look out!' yelled Mervin. The red balloon was floating straight towards a prickly holly bush.

'Pop!' The balloon burst, but to everyone's surprise the little owl laughed, flapped his wings even harder and flew higher into the sky. He had learnt to fly at last!

Orlando was so happy that he took Mervin and Matthew home to tea. Mrs Owl gave them ham and eggs and fruit cake. The little owl did not want any tea. He was still flying happily far, far above the wood.

A Dog and his Reflection

There was once a dog who stole a piece of meat from a butcher's shop. The dog was very pleased with himself and went running away over a little bridge holding the meat in his mouth.

But half-way over the bridge the dog saw a reflection of himself in the water. He did not understand about reflections and thought it was another dog with a juicy piece of meat. And as he was a very greedy dog, as well as being naughty, he wanted the second piece of meat as well.

So he snapped at it – and dropped the meat he was carrying into the water, where the current carried it away. So the silly, greedy dog had no meat at all.

The Scarecrow and the Tortoise

Sammy the scarecrow was a very fine scarecrow. He had a splendid straw hat with a feather in it, a bright red jacket and black and white checked trousers.

But Sammy was lonely. He stood in the middle of a big field, looking after it for the farmer. He was proud because the farmer had given him such an important job, but it was lonely in the big field all day and all night.

Sammy tried to make friends with the birds that flew busily here and there. He would call to them as they flew by, but they were frightened by Sammy and did not know he just wanted a friend to talk to now and again.

One day a family of rabbits came to play near Sammy. He called to them, 'Please rabbits, will you come and play with me?'

The rabbits bounded over to Sammy.

'My name is Sammy,' he said.

'Hello Sammy,' said the rabbits. 'Would you like to play hide-and-seek?'

'Oh yes please,' said Sammy. 'I've never played hide-and-seek before though. You will have to show me how to do it.'

'You run away and hide. We come to look for you,' explained the biggest rabbit.

'But I can't run away and hide,' said Sammy. 'I can't move.'

The rabbits all laughed.

'You can't move! Well you are a funny creature.' And they all bounded off and left Sammy feeling even more lonely.

The next day a little boy was walking along the path at the edge of the field. He stopped by the fence to look at Sammy and then he waved to him. But poor

Sammy couldn't wave back. The little boy gave up waving and turned and ran off down the path.

To Sammy's delight, the little boy came back the next day. He stood and watched Sammy as before, then waved and ran off. Soon the little boy came every day.

Sammy enjoyed these visits but he still felt lonely. If only he could talk to the little boy, or find a real friend.

One morning he was standing half asleep in the sun when he felt a nudge at his feet. He looked down to see a sleepy tortoise.

'Hello,' said the tortoise, yawning. 'I'm sorry to bother you. But I have to settle down for my winter snooze. I like somewhere warm and comfortable where I know I will not be disturbed. Would you mind very much if I stop here by your feet?'

'But of course,' Sammy said. 'I'd be pleased to have you. I can look after you and keep you warm all winter.'

'Thanks,' said the tortoise, yawning again, hardly able to keep his eyes open.

'But . . . what made you think of coming here?' asked Sammy.

'Oh I belong to Timothy, the little boy who comes to see you. He thought you might not mind.'

Sammy looked over at the fence and saw Timothy, waving happily. Sammy felt very happy. Timothy must have understood after all about Sammy not being able to wave back, and he had sent him a friend.

'What's your name?' Sammy asked quickly, because the tortoise was nearly asleep.

'Tom,' the tortoise mumbled sleepily. 'Perhaps we can be friends when I wake up in the spring.' Then he fell asleep.

All through the winter, Sammy kept Tom warm. He was happy. It was nice to have a friend at last!

Grasshopper Music

Long, long ago, the first grasshopper in the world was feeling rather sad. All the other creatures it knew could make their own special noise. The birds could sing, the frogs could croak, and the mice could squeak. Green Grasshopper couldn't make any noise at all.

Then, one day, when Green Grasshopper was out for a walk in a wood, he saw two tiny men just about his own size. They were each carrying a little wooden case.

'Why, those tiny men must be pixies,' thought Green Grasshopper.

He had heard about the little fairy-folk who lived in those parts.

'I wonder where they are going, and what they are going to do with those cases,' he thought.

Green Grasshopper followed the pixies until they came, at last, to a small clearing in a wood. There, they opened their wooden cases, and each one took out a tiny fiddle and a tiny bow. The pixies were soon playing a jolly tune. Green

Grasshopper had never seen or heard a fiddle before, so he was very excited. He couldn't keep his feet still, and he asked the pixies if he could dance to their music.

'Of course! Of course!' beamed the pixies, pleased that Green Grasshopper liked their music.

Green Grasshopper began to dance, and soon other pixies appeared, and danced to the music, too. The fiddlers played many tunes and they all had a very happy afternoon together. At last, it was time for the grasshopper to leave. He said good-bye to the pixies, and hurried away through the wood to find his friend, the second grasshopper in the world. His name was George.

'George! George!' called Green Grass-hopper. 'I've been listening to some fairy fiddlers, and they made such lovely music.'

'Fiddlers!' said George, in surprise. 'What are fiddlers, and what did they do? I've never heard of them.'

Green Grasshopper found it difficult to explain.

'Look,' he said to George, 'I will show you what I mean. Just pretend, for a moment, that my right wing is the funny box thing, and my left wing is the stick. Now, I scrape my left wing across my right wing, like this.'

Green Grasshopper scraped away, and was surprised to find that he made a funny chirping noise. It didn't sound quite like a fiddle, but George thought it was a very jolly noise, and he began to

dance to it – a jumpy, jerky sort of dance. Then George tried rubbing his left wing across his right wing, and he found that he could make the same sort of noise as Green Grasshopper. They stopped and looked at each other in amazement, then began again, scraping away together.

'We're playing a tune,' chuckled the grasshoppers happily, 'a grasshopper tune! We must teach the third grass-hopper in the world, and the fourth, how to do it, too. Then we can all play together.'

Ever since that far off time, grasshop-pers have taught each other how to play the funny grasshopper tune. In meadows, in the summer-time, folk can hear them making their own special grasshopper music.

Perhaps *you* will hear them, one day!

Bimbo Flies Away

It was a bright, sunny day and Amanda was cleaning Bimbo's cage. While she was working, the little budgerigar fluttered out through the open window into the old apple tree in the garden. From there, he could look right out over the lush, green countryside.

'Amanda won't miss me while I fly to that farm over there,' thought Bimbo, taking off gracefully into the air.

He landed in a leafy bush in the middle of a field.

'Hee-haw, hee-haw!' Standing nearby was a big, furry donkey.

'Welcome to my field little bird,' said the donkey. 'Make yourself at home.'

'Thank you Donkey, but I'm afraid I can't stay. I must be moving on.'

'Very well,' replied the donkey, 'but be sure you have a word with my friend Goat before you go. He's next door.'

'Hello,' called Bimbo cheerfully, as he flew into Goat's pen.

'Very nice of you to call,' said Goat. You don't have to leave straight away do you? Make yourself comfortable.'

'Well,' said Bimbo, 'I *should* go home to Amanda . . . but . . . I will stay and have lunch with you first.'

'Delighted!' said Goat as Bimbo flew down and settled on the straw by his feet.

Read about Bimbo's next adventure in the countryside on page 104.

The Lion Who Wanted an Umbrella

The lion growled angrily as he looked at himself in the pool. His long, tawny mane was curly again.

'Every time it rains, my mane goes curly!' he said. 'I need an umbrella.'

An elephant was drinking at the other side of the pool. He overheard the lion. 'Well, I haven't an umbrella, but if you scratch my back for me with your sharp claws, I'll give you something as good.'

The lion took another look at his mane, and hurried over to scratch the elephant's back.

'Thank you, lion', said the elephant. 'This should stop your mane from getting wet.'

He held out a basket in his trunk. 'I found it. Put it over your head.'

The lion put the basket over his head and turned to look at himself in the pool . . . SPLASH! . . . The basket certainly kept the lion's head dry. The only trouble was, he couldn't see a thing!

'If there's one thing I hate more than a wet mane, it's wet feet,' he said.

A fierce-looking alligator floated up to him. 'Wet feet, did you say? I have the very thing.' The alligator disappeared for a moment, then came up with a pair of wellington boots in his sharp teeth.

The lion tried on the wellingtons. They seemed quite comfortable. He gave the basket to the alligator in exchange and marched off into the jungle.

He hadn't gone far when he heard his friend roaring to him across the jungle. He began to run towards the sound . . . CRASH! . . . The wellingtons tripped him up. As he lay there rubbing his sore nose, he saw a mouse staring at him in surprise.

'Whatever are you doing?' she squeaked. 'I've never seen a lion dancing before.'

'I'm not dancing!' growled the lion crossly. 'These wellingtons tripped me up and I've hurt my nose.'

Before the lion could gather himself up, the mouse had scurried under a tree and popped up with a scarf.

'Put this round your nose,' she suggested kindly. 'I've been using it for a nest, but if you give me the wellingtons, you can have it.'

The lion took the scarf gratefully, and tied it round his sore nose. He watched as the mouse ordered her family into the wellingtons, then set off once more.

He could hardly believe his eyes when a cheeky hare jumped up in front of him and grinned. Usually he could smell hares long before he could see them.

'If I can't smell hares, how shall I catch my supper?' he declared, tearing off the scarf.

Thinking of his supper made him feel hungry, so he began to sniff around. 'What's that shiny red stuff over there?' he muttered to himself. It was a jelly left under a tree to cool.

The lion was so hungry by this time that he was ready to eat anything. He put his paw into the bowl and tried to scoop it up, but the red jelly slithered through his sharp claws. He put his mouth down to the bowl, but his teeth were too big to fit inside.

He dipped his tail into the jelly, then chased round and round himself trying to lick it off. Finally, exhausted, he fell asleep with his claws around the bowl of slippery jelly.

As soon as the lion was asleep, Biffy the monkey tiptoed towards the jelly. As he bent down to eat it, his big straw sun-hat tickled the lion's nose, and wakened him.

'Grrrr!' roared the lion fiercely. The little monkey jumped away and scrambled up a tree. He didn't even stop when his straw hat fell to the ground.

The angry lion stood at the foot of the tree, glaring around him. Then he spotted the monkey's big hat.

'Just the thing,' he said to himself as he picked it up. 'This will keep my mane dry even better than an umbrella.' Forgetting all about the monkey, he hurried away. Just then it began to rain.

The Nightingale

Long ago, the Emperor of China lived in a fine palace. People came from all over the world to see it. All of them said that the loveliest thing in the palace was the little Nightingale which sang in the high trees of the Emperor's garden. The garden ran down to the seashore and the poor fishermen casting their nets would stop work to listen. But no-one had ever told the Emperor about the Nightingale in the wood.

Then one day he read about it in a book. 'Why have I never seen this bird?' he asked, and sent for his servant to question him.

He ordered the Nightingale to be brought to him but the servant did not know where it was.

The servant ran upstairs and downstairs through the palace, and half the court ran with him, but no-one had heard of the Nightingale, or knew where she lived.

'There must be someone who knows,' wailed the servant in despair.

Then at last they found a kitchen-maid who had heard of the Nightingale.

'Yes, I know her very well,' she said. 'She lives in the high trees of the wood down by the sea.'

'Take us to her,' said the servant, 'and you shall be rewarded by the Emperor himself.'

So the kitchen-maid took them down to the wood by the sea and the Nightingale sang for them. The servant

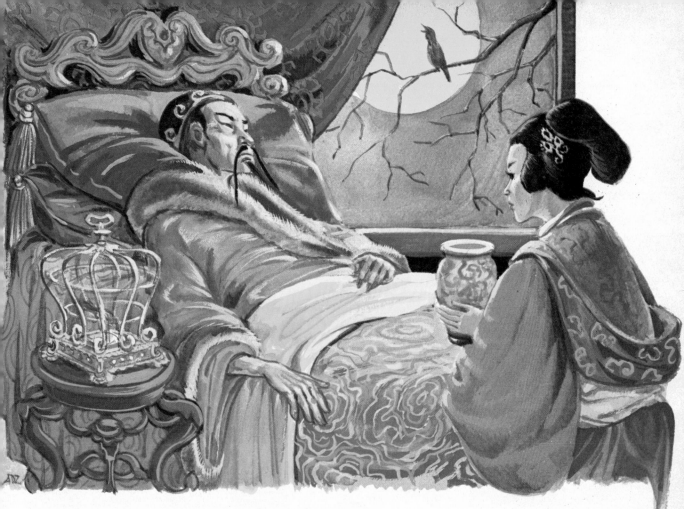

invited the bird to sing for the Emperor.

'I shall be very pleased to do so,' said the Nightingale. 'I will come to the palace tomorrow evening.'

The Nightingale came and sang for the Emperor as she had promised. The tears ran down the Emperor's cheeks for the song was so beautiful. Afterwards the Emperor would not let the Nightingale go back to the woods.

One day a large parcel arrived. In the box was an artificial Nightingale covered with precious stones. When it was wound up it could sing one of the tunes that the real Nightingale sang. The Emperor and the Court were delighted and everyone forgot the real Nightingale, who went back to her home in the woods.

The artificial bird continued singing for a year. One evening when the Emperor was in bed there was a sudden

bang, buzz, fuzz, and the bird stopped singing its pretty song.

The Emperor called in his Chief Physician and a watchmaker but, although they tried very hard, they could not mend the bird properly.

The Emperor fell ill and everyone was afraid he might die. One night he saw and heard the real Nightingale singing on the branch of a tree outside his window.

He was so happy that he fell into a deep sleep, and when the courtiers came to see him in the morning he was quite well. The Emperor called for the real Nightingale and begged her to stay at the palace. The Nightingale agreed so long as she was free to come and go as she wished. So, every evening from then on, the Nightingale came to the Emperor's palace and sang from the branch of a tree outside his window.

65

Sweet Woodland Music

'Isn't it quiet since the Nightingale family left us!' sighed sleepy Dormouse, munching a hazel-nut.

'Willie Warbler has flown away, too,' snuffled Hedgehog, waddling through the crisp, dry leaves.

'That's a sign that I shall soon have to start making my house cosy for winter!' nodded Mole, as he dug in the soil for worms and grubs.

Dormouse busied himself collecting a bundle of leaves and grass. 'I miss the sweet songs that the birds used to sing to us,' he squeaked.

'Me, too!' agreed Hedgehog and Mole.

The big Water Rat, who was listening to the conversation as he sat by the woodland stream, scratched his fur thoughtfully. Suddenly, he swished his tail excitedly in the water. He knew how to fill the woodland air with sweet music again.

Scampering round the water reeds which grew thickly in the stream, he chose one tall reed. With his sharp teeth he bit it into six small pieces. Each piece was a different size, and the smallest was very, very small. Carefully, Water Rat sucked the soft, juicy sap from the inside of the pieces of reed.

By now, Water Rat had an audience. Wise Toad hopped about croaking, 'What are you making, Water Rat?'

'You'll see in a few minutes,' said Water Rat, binding the pieces of reed tightly together with strips of bark from a silver birch tree.

Wise Toad was excited. His croaks were heard by all the creatures of the wood and they came scurrying to the stream from all directions.

Water Rat beamed shyly at all his visitors.

'Here is something which, I hope, will bring you all happiness during the coming autumn days!' he said quietly.

Putting the pipes to his mouth, he blew softly into them. The air was filled with the sweetest music the animals had ever heard.

'It sounds just like Nightingale singing over the water,' murmured sleepy Dormouse to snuffling Hedgehog, as he munched another hazel-nut. They knew that winter would be a much happier time now that they had some music.

66

Busy Beavers

Granny was looking after Peter while Mummy was out. She had brought a big calendar for Peter to see. It had coloured pictures of different parts of the world and Peter liked it very much. He turned the pages carefully. They looked at a picture of Switzerland with mountains and snow, and a picture of Africa with lions and tigers.

'Where's that?' asked Peter, pointing to a picture of a blue lake and dark trees. 'And what's the animal swimming in the water?'

'That's a beaver, in Canada,' said Granny. I lived out there a long time ago when I was a girl.'

The beaver in Granny's picture was a dark brown animal with a long, flat tail.

'He's bigger than my cat,' said Peter. 'Why has he got sticks in his mouth?'

'He's building a dam in the water,' replied Granny. 'He's very clever. Would you like me to tell you about him?'

'Yes, please,' said Peter, snuggling on to Granny's lap to listen.

'Well,' said Granny, 'beavers are very hard workers and they are busy all day long.'

'Like Mummy,' said Peter.

'That's right,' said Granny. 'Shall I go on and tell you some more about them?'

'Yes please,' said Peter. 'What are they busy doing?'

'They gnaw the trees down and use them to build dams across the river, and they make their houses with sticks,' Granny continued. 'Their houses are called lodges. They swim along with sticks and branches that they have cut down with their sharp teeth.'

'That's clever,' said Peter admiringly. 'What do they eat?'

'They like the bark of trees best,' said Granny. 'So they gnaw away at the trees a lot of the time.'

Peter pulled a face. 'I'm glad I'm not a beaver – I'd hate to eat bark,' he said. 'But I'd like the swimming part. Do their big tails get in the way when they're swimming?'

'I expect their tails help,' said Granny. 'And they can smack them on the water to raise the alarm if there's danger.'

'They're clever animals,' said Peter.

'They are,' said Granny. 'And they work hard from sunrise to sunset. I expect they're glad to go to sleep in their house on the water.'

'Did you like living in Canada?' asked Peter.

'Well enough,' replied Granny. 'But it was a long time ago.'

'Then I'll draw you a picture of a beaver,' said Peter. 'It will help you to remember more about it.'

Dog on a Swing

Ben skipped across the fresh, dewy grass in the park, whistling a merry tune.

'Miaow . . . miaow,' sang Bill the Siamese cat, as he scampered along by Ben's side.

'What a clever cat you are, Bill!' said Ben in the middle of his tune. 'You must be the only singing cat in the world.'

They came to a little hill that was covered with pretty pink flowers. Bill ran on ahead, singing and sniffing and twitching his whiskers as he bounced through the sweet-smelling flowers.

When he reached the top of the hill, Bill stopped by a big tree and stared.

'Well, fancy that!' he said to himself. 'There's a dog having a swing.'

And he sat amongst the flowers and watched and grinned, because he thought the dog looked so funny.

'Bill,' called Ben, as he came up. 'I've been looking for you . . .' Then his eyes opened wide as he saw the big, furry collie dog swinging happily to and fro. Holding the collie's lead was a little girl with long fair hair. She wore the biggest hat he had ever seen.

'Hello,' said Ben, stepping out from behind the tree. 'My name's Ben and this is Bill.'

The little girl looked up shyly and said, 'My name's Beatrice and that's my dog on the swing. She's called Bella. She's very clever you know.'

'Bill's clever too – he can sing,' said Ben proudly.

Beatrice looked thoughtful. 'Isn't it funny,' she said, 'that all our names start with 'B' – Bill, Ben, Bella and Beatrice.'

'That's because we're all so clever,' laughed Ben, as they ran off through the park together.

The Giraffe Who Hated being Tall

'I've never seen an animal that looks as silly as I do,' complained Gervais, the baby giraffe, as he looked at his reflection in the river. 'My legs are too long, and so is my neck. I look like a leopard with an ostrich's neck, walking on stilts! Ugh!'

'Long legs help you to run fast,' said his mother, quietly.

'The antelopes have quite short legs,' said Gervais, 'and they can run faster than we can.'

'And with your long neck you can see danger coming,' his mother went on.

'Yes, and lions and leopards and cheetahs can see *us* from a long way off,' said Gervais. 'Look at the wild pigs. They can run about in the long grass without anyone seeing them.'

Gervais's mother sighed. She knew that he would learn his lesson one day.

Soon the dry season came. The hot sun shone like a fire every day, and no rain fell. Soon the tall grasses of the plain began to dry up. All the animals of the plain whispered to each other, 'It's time for us to move.'

So they began their journey. They walked over the hot, dusty plain towards the mountains they could see far away in the distance.

'It will be cooler there,' they said, 'and we shall find plenty of grass.'

But the mountains were further away than they looked. Day after day the animals kept walking. All the time the sun became hotter, the grass drier and the animals hungrier.

Now the lions and leopards and cheetahs could see the antelopes and wild pigs easily, for there was no long grass to hide them. And the antelopes were too tired to run fast.

But, Gervais had plenty to eat. With his long legs and long neck, he was able to reach the green leaves at the very tops of the trees. None of the other animals could stretch as far as that.

'Aren't you glad you have long legs and a long neck?' said his mother.

And as they were kind giraffes, they pulled down some of the green branches so that the antelopes could eat the leaves.

The Clumsy Dinosaur

Millions of years ago, there was a tiny spot in the middle of an egg. The little spot grew and grew until, at last, it popped out of its shell. It was called a dinosaur.

From the moment he took his first peep at the world, Dubby Dinosaur nibbled away at plants and, as the days and months went by, he ate so much, that he grew to an animal of tremendous size.

Dubby Dinosaur had a splendid view of everything around him because he was so tall. But, being so big, he was also very clumsy, and if there was anything lying in his way, he would either trip over it or squash it flat.

'Really,' his mother would exclaim, 'you *are* a careless fellow! Why don't you look where you are going?' But Dubby would only laugh. His laughter was so loud that it shook all the leaves off the trees.

One day, when he had laughed and the leaves had fallen off the trees, he heard a squeak coming from beneath a pile of leaves.

Dubby bent down and was surprised to see a tiny spider creep out. The spider looked him straight in the eye, and said angrily, 'You clumsy old dinosaur, you noisy old dinosaur, just who do you think you are?' Dubby could hardly believe his ears. No-one had ever dared to scold a dinosaur before, and he admired the little creature's courage. He was too surprised to argue back.

'I could puff you into the sky with one blow,' roared Dubby, 'but because I think you are a very brave little fellow, I would like us to be friends.'

From that moment on, clumsy Dubby took special care when he went walking, because he didn't want to tread on his little friend.

The Dancing Tail

It was a hot, sleepy afternoon deep in the Australian bush and most folk were dozing. The koala family had wedged themselves comfortably in the branches of a eucalyptus tree. Two brown wallabies were resting in the shade of some bushes while nearby, a little lizard called a gecko had settled himself on a smooth, round rock at the foot of a pine tree.

Everyone had settled down for a nap except for one beady-eyed, sharp-beaked fellow who was wide-awake. It was Kookaburra. He was perched on a low branch of a eucalyptus tree, staring very hard at somebody near the ground. And that somebody was Gecko!

Kookaburra had watched Gecko run through the undergrowth, stopping now and then to catch a fly or two with his long, sticky tongue. He had watched Gecko climb on to the rock just below the branch he was sitting on. Then, to his delight, Kookaburra had watched Gecko fall sound asleep.

'Mm,' thought Kookaburra. 'Plump little lizards are delicious and I haven't had my lunch yet.' And, chuckling to himself, Kookaburra edged his way along the branch until he was right over the rock poor Gecko was lying on,

then . . . *whooosh*, Kookaburra swooped. But then, *thwack*! Kookaburra's beak smacked the rock, for Gecko had disappeared.

The very moment Kookaburra had left his branch, Gecko had scuttled off the rock as fast as his little legs could carry him. He ran for his life through the undergrowth, over tree stumps and under bracken. He ran and ran until he felt quite sure he was out of Kookaburra's reach and stopped, at last, by a fallen tree.

It was then he discovered that something was missing. Gecko knew he had lost something very important.

A galah flew by and perched on the fallen tree. 'Good-day,' greeted the handsome pink and grey bird. 'I say, you look a bit upset. What's wrong?'

Gecko looked at the galah with his large round eyes and blinked away a tear. 'I-I-I've lost m-m-my *tail*,' sniffed Gecko. And he turned round to show the bird where his tail had been.

'My hat!' said the galah. 'So you have. Well, cheer up, I'll help you look for it. What colour is it?'

Gecko thought for a moment. 'It's a bit difficult to say,' he began. 'You see I . . . that is my tail, too, of course . . .

seem to change colour depending where I am or what I'm sitting on.'

'Well, what *were* you sitting on when you lost it?' asked the galah helpfully.

'A rock,' said Gecko. 'A sunny, honey-coloured rock.'

'Right,' said the galah. 'I'll fly back to the rock and see if I can find your tail. You follow on and catch me up.'

'Oh, thank you,' said Gecko, feeling better already. 'You are a kind bird.'

It wasn't difficult to find the rock, for when the galah arrived, there was quite a crowd of animals standing around it. They were all chattering excitedly.

'Make way, make way,' called the galah. 'I've come to look for some lost property. Has anyone seen a sunny . . . no, a *honey*-coloured tail around here, belonging to a gecko?'

'I should just think we have,' grunted a wombat shuffling out of the crowd. 'Have a look.'

And there, dancing about on top of the rock, all by itself, was Gecko's tail!

'My hat!' exclaimed the galah. 'Now I've seen everything.'

'You see,' explained a wallaby, 'a gecko is a very clever creature. Whenever he is in real danger he can shed his tail and run for his life. The tail that is left behind does a little dance to trick whoever is chasing the gecko into thinking he has caught him. Later on, the gecko grows a new tail to replace the one he has lost.'

Just as the wallaby had finished speaking, Gecko appeared.

'What a trick!' said Gecko, who had been listening. 'I will remember that in future.'

And, a little way off, Kookaburra who was sitting in a tree nursing a very sore beak said, 'And so will I!'

Timothy Squirrel
Catches Cold

Timothy Squirrel opened his eyes and yawned. He was still very young and his tiny bed was warm and cosy.

The little squirrel blinked. He sniffed and his whiskers twitched, then he rolled over to the side of his bed. He stood on his back legs and held on to the window ledge with his paws.

Then Timothy peeped over the top. What a strange world it was!

All Timothy could see were branches of trees. They were all covered with strange white stuff. Timothy opened the front door and peeped out inquisitively. Suddenly, he heard his mother's voice just behind him.

'Come inside, Timothy,' she called. 'You will catch a cold if you go out into the snow.'

'Snow?' cried Timothy. 'What is snow?'

'It is that white stuff outside,' explained Mother Squirrel. 'And it is very cold. Now I am going out for a few minutes to collect some nuts from the store. Be very good and stay in your warm bed.'

Timothy nodded and jumped back into bed.

When his mother had gone, Timothy uncurled and looked out of the door again. Big, white snowflakes were fluttering down all around him.

Timothy Squirrel was so excited that he climbed a little too high. Suddenly he lost his balance and fell with a plop right into the soft, white snow.

Just then, Mother Squirrel came along. She heard Timothy's squeals and carried him up to the nest.

Timothy Squirrel was very wet and cold, and was glad to be tucked into his bed of leaves and moss. Mother Squirrel did not scold. Instead she said, 'I think you'll be sorry you did not do as you were told.'

And sure enough, a day or two later, a very miserable little squirrel sat up in bed under plenty of warm blankets, and all he could say was, '*A-a-a-tishoo!*'

The Cat Who Liked to Stay at Home

Sometimes Tania went to visit her Granny, who lived in a cosy little cottage at the other end of the village. Granny sat in her armchair on one side of the fire. And on the other side, in another armchair, sat Jumbo, Granny's cat. Jumbo was a very handsome cat, but he was also lazy and enjoyed his comforts.

'Move him out of the chair and sit down, Tania,' Granny would say.

So Tania would gather Jumbo up in her arms and put him down gently on the hearth-rug.

'There! You sit there,' she would tell him.

Jumbo would curl up, just where she put him, and go straight to sleep again. He would stay there, sleeping, all the time that Tania was talking to Granny. As soon as she got up to go home, Jumbo would wake up enough to jump back into the armchair. Then he would go to sleep again.

'I never saw such a lazy cat,' declared Granny. 'I need never fear about him wandering away and getting lost. He never goes farther than the hedge at the bottom of the garden.'

One day, Tania and her mother and father went for a long walk. They walked right through the forest, and found themselves in fields on the far side.

As they were walking across the fields, Tania caught sight of a large, reddish animal slinking into a hedge.

'Ooo, is that a fox?' she exclaimed.

'Let's go and see,' said her father.

So they hurried to the hedge. Dad pulled aside some bushes and they peered in. At first it was too gloomy to see anything. Then something moved, and they found themselves looking at a huge cat.

'Why, it's Jumbo!' exclaimed Tania.

'So it is,' said Dad.

'Jumbo! Jumbo! Puss-puss-puss! Come here!' called Tania.

But Jumbo just looked at her as though he had never seen her before, and then turned away.

Tania was disappointed.

'I don't think he even knows me,' she said sadly.

'He doesn't want to,' said Dad. 'Cats are nice, cuddly animals when they are at home by the fire, but when they are out in the woods and hedges they become wild creatures again. Do you see his eyes glowing? They're the eyes of a wild hunter, looking for its prey. Mice!'

They moved back from the hedge, leaving Jumbo to his hunting.

'I don't think I like him so much when he's in this mood,' said Tania.

'Well,' said her father, smiling, 'it's all part of being a cat.'

Lucky Piggy

'I do wish someone would buy me,' sighed the pig pencil-sharpener in the toy-shop window. 'I have been sitting on this shelf longer than any of you other toys.'

At that moment, they saw a little girl outside the window. Mr Chuff, the engine, moved nearer to the front of the shelf. Mr Golliwog puffed out his chest and sat up very straight and tall. The Fairy Doll shook her wings to make them sparkle, but the little girl did not look at them.

Piggy grunted and glowed almost bright red as he tried to get closer to the window.

'That's what I want, Mummy,' the little girl told the lady who had stopped beside her. 'I want that piggy pencil-sharpener.'

'Then you shall have him, Rosemary,' her Mummy said. 'But you can choose something else as well as the piggy for your birthday.'

'Thank you,' said Rosemary, smiling happily. 'Then I should like coloured pencils and books with pictures that I can colour.'

'Let's wait a little longer before buying them. There are six weeks to go before your birthday,' her Mummy smiled. 'You know, you may decide you would like something else by that time.'

'I don't think I shall want anything different,' Rosemary said quickly. 'Piggy is so jolly, and useful too.'

Piggy was happy at last. Rosemary wanted him, and she was a nice little girl. Every Saturday the little girl peered in Mrs Puppet's window and gave Piggy a smile.

Then on the fifth Saturday, just after Rosemary had smiled at Piggy and gone home again, a lady came into Mrs Puppet's shop and said that she wanted to buy lots of toys.

The lady said, 'I want small toys for the Garden Fête Lucky Dip.'

'Then I'll fetch the toys that have been on my shelves for ages,' Mrs Puppet said.

The lady smiled as Mrs Puppet put plastic boats, rubber elephants, clock-work cars, games and puzzles on the counter. Suddenly Piggy felt himself tugged off the shelf and put on top of the pile.

'Oh, no! Not me, please,' he squeaked. 'Rosemary is coming for me very soon.'

But no one took any notice of him and he was pushed into a paper bag.

Much later Piggy was wrapped in green paper and pushed into a big tub full of curly wood shavings.

Next day the tub was taken to a park and from inside the tub Piggy heard laughing, singing and talking. Lots of fingers pushed and prodded him. But nobody pulled him out of the tub.

'This is worse than being on Mrs Puppet's shelf,' he grunted. 'I shall go rusty and useless if somebody does not find me soon.'

Then, suddenly, Piggy felt himself being lifted out of the tub.

As the green paper was pulled away from him, Piggy blinked in the sunshine.

'Oh, my piggy sharpener!' a voice said. 'Fancy finding you here when I thought I should never see you again! This is the luckiest dip I have ever had.'

'It's Rosemary!' Piggy squeaked excitedly. 'What a wonderful surprise! I belong to Rosemary at last.'

Princess Tania's Beautiful Present

Princess Tania thought she was the most beautiful princess in the world. She was spoilt and vain and she loved to look at herself in the mirror. She even admired her reflection in her porridge spoon.

On her birthday the courtiers and servants brought presents of jewellery and clothes, hair ribbons and fine slippers.

But the palace gardener was a wise young man. He told the Princess that his present was out in the palace gardens.

Princess Tania ran outside to see what it could be. A tree filled with fruit, or a fountain, or a swing where she could read and eat sweets all day . . .

But all she found on the lawn was an ordinary bird standing half-hidden in the trees by the lake, eyeing her solemnly. The Princess was angry. 'I don't want you for a present,' she cried, stamping her foot. 'You're not nearly grand enough for me.'

'Look in the water at your reflection,' said the bird. 'Then we'll see who's beautiful.'

Princess Tania looked in the lake, but all she could see was an ugly, cross face.

'That's not me,' she said. 'Where have I gone to?' She leaned over the water to see – and fell right in. Crying and angry, the Princess stood in the water, her fine clothes dripping wet. She pulled the weeds from her hair to throw them at the bird, then in surprise she said, 'Why,

you're not an ordinary bird at all. You're a Royal Peacock – you're beautiful!'

The peacock had come out from the trees and his huge coloured tail was like a jewelled fan. He looked very stately and royal.

'Well, how do you like your present, little Princess?' asked the gardener, appearing beside them.

'It's a wonderful present,' said the Princess, feeling sorry and ashamed for being rude and cross. 'It's much more beautiful than I am. In fact, I don't think I'm very beautiful at all.'

After that, the Princess and the gardener and the peacock became great friends. The Princess stopped trying to be beautiful and learned how to be friendly and kind instead. In fact, the young gardener liked her so much that he asked her to marry him, and they looked after the peacock together.

A Very Vain Bunny

Beatrice Bunny had a new coat. It was a bright red one, with six brass buttons down the front. She was very proud of her coat and several times a day she would peep into her mirror. Soon she started wearing ribbons and beads of many colours.

At last Beatrice Bunny became so vain that the rest of the woodland people would not speak to her. It was not long before she was walking along with her head in the air and stopping to peep into all the ponds and puddles of water.

One day Beatrice was wandering through the woods when she passed a few of the woodland people. She lifted her head high as she walked by.

Freddie Flopears giggled and that made Beatrice lift her head even higher. Can you guess what happened then?

Beatrice walked straight into a big stone, tripped over it and fell head first into a pond of very muddy water.

The woodland people laughed and laughed as Beatrice flapped and spluttered and slithered about in the mud.

'What about the wonderful red coat now?' cried Horace Hedgehog. 'I'm sure it will shrink.'

Beatrice struggled tearfully to climb out of the pond, but she had to be helped by the other animals. Then, because they were really very kind-hearted, they took her home to get dry.

Strangely enough, the red coat disappeared and was never seen again. Johnny Moptail said it had gone rusty. Clarence, the fox-cub, thought it might have caught cold. Everyone agreed that Beatrice was much nicer without it.

The Fairy Over the Pond

One summer day, Jenny and her big brother James went to the pond near their home with their fishing nets, hoping to catch some sticklebacks. The pond was a very interesting place – there were snails, tadpoles and frogs to look for, and pretty flowers growing around the edge.

'There's a stickleback,' said James, pointing excitedly to a little fish darting in and out of the weeds. He dragged his net through the water but the stickleback disappeared underneath it.

'Bother,' said James and tried again. This time the stickleback swam right in, but just as James lifted his net, it swam out again. James felt cross. 'They always get away,' he grumbled.

'There's another one – let me try,' said Jenny. But she couldn't reach far enough. The stickleback had gone under the weeds and only a few small bubbles showed where he had been. Jenny put down her net and tried feeling for him with her hands. She ran her fingers gently through the cool water but all she could feel was the tangled pond weed.

'Let's try together, with both nets,' suggested James, and as another stickleback swam into view, they held hands and leaned over the water with their nets close together. But the nets got caught up with each other and the children slithered about. James grabbed Jenny's arm and Jenny caught hold of James' shirt, but they couldn't stop their feet from sliding in.

'Oh dear! My sandals are all wet and muddy,' said Jenny.

'Look at my socks,' said James. 'Let's take them off and put them in the sun to dry.'

The sun felt lovely on the children's bare feet. They both picked up their fishing nets and ran about on the warm grass to see if they could catch any butterflies instead of sticklebacks.

'James!' called Jenny from beside the pond. 'Look over there. There's a fairy. I saw a fairy! It flew over the pond!'

James came running to look but the fairy flew further away. 'I wish it would come nearer,' said James. 'I'd love to catch it in my net. Do you think it would talk to us?'

'You mustn't catch fairies,' said Jenny in a whisper. 'They're magic and you can't touch magic. But perhaps it will fly back so that we can see it properly.'

'Did it have fairy wings?' asked James.

'Yes,' said Jenny. 'They were silver and nearly invisible. Oh look! Here it comes again.'

The fairy flew towards them, hovering in the sunlight, and darting up and down. It had a long, blue-green body and transparent, vibrating wings.

'That's not a fairy,' said James scornfully. 'That's a dragonfly! We learned all about them at school. They only live by ponds, and they go out flying when it's sunny. They zoom about looking for insects and . . .'

But Jenny wasn't listening. She was watching fascinated as the dragonfly hovered, then skimmed past her gracefully, its coloured body a sheen of green and blue-black.

'It's lovely,' breathed Jenny.

'It's a beautiful insect,' said James admiringly. 'We drew pictures of them at school and looked at drawings of them in books, but it's much more fun seeing a real one. Doesn't it whizz along fast!' Then he remembered he was cross at losing his sticklebacks.

'I knew all along it couldn't really be a fairy,' he said. 'Anyway, it looks much more like a helicopter. I'm going to see if my shoes are dry.'

He shouldered his fishing net and walked away but Jenny stayed by the pond for a few more minutes to watch the dragonfly. She knew James was probably right and it wasn't a fairy, but it still had a special magic about it.

Grey Rabbit

Grey Rabbit had big feet, long, silken ears and soft, grey fur. He belonged to a little boy named Stewart and lived in a very big hutch. The hutch stood inside a shed at the bottom of Stewart's garden.

Stewart loved Grey Rabbit and every day went to feed him and give him clean drinking water.

One day when Stewart was preparing Grey Rabbit's dinner in the shed, his friend Jeremy came in. Jeremy wanted Stewart to go out to play with him.

Stewart said good-bye to Grey Rabbit and told him he would be back soon.

Grey Rabbit sat all alone in his big hutch and wondered what he should do. First, he hopped round his hutch. Then, he climbed up the wire at the front of his hutch and twitched his nose. Suddenly, he remembered he had not eaten his dinner. Stewart had forgotten to feed him. He hopped round his hutch again. Then he sat down beside the door. He looked at the door and gave it a push with his nose. It opened. The floor of the shed looked a long way down. Grey Rabbit sat and looked at the floor and then he jumped. He landed safely on some sacks. He walked all round the shed, looking and sniffing for something to eat. There was nothing for his dinner in the shed.

Poor Grey Rabbit was feeling very hungry now. He hopped out of the shed and looked around. All he could see were lots of pretty flowers, but Grey Rabbit wanted some tasty lettuces or carrots to eat.

Grey Rabbit hopped along the garden path until he came to the gate, and he just managed to squeeze underneath. He had never been outside the gate before and he did not know which way to turn.

He waited until there were no cars coming, then he hurried across the road. First he saw lots of houses, but past the houses Grey Rabbit could see something green. Off he went, hopping quickly towards it. As he came nearer he saw it was a very thick, high hedge and finding a small hole in it, he slipped through.

Grey Rabbit found himself in a farm-yard and saw ducks swimming on a pond. He was going to speak to them when he heard a loud mooing sound. He was frightened. He had never heard a cow before, so he did not stop to speak to the ducks, but hopped straight through the farmyard and into a field at the other side.

The field was very green and he was sure he would find something to eat there. Then, just as he began to look around, he heard a voice he knew. It was Stewart's voice. Stewart and Jeremy were walking towards him. Grey Rabbit was so pleased that he thumped his big feet on the ground, waved his ears and hopped up to Stewart.

Stewart said, 'Hello, Grey Rabbit. What are you doing here?' Then he gently picked him up. He put Grey Rabbit inside his coat, to keep him warm, and they all set off for home.

When they got home Stewart put lettuce leaves, a small carrot and some clean water in the rabbit hutch. Then he put Grey Rabbit back inside his hutch and made sure that the door was shut properly this time. Stewart and Jeremy said good-bye to him and then went off to play again.

When they had gone, Grey Rabbit ate the carrot and the lettuce leaves and drank a little water.

He was very pleased to be home again. He washed his face and whiskers and his muddy feet, then he lay down, closed his eyes, twitched his nose and fell fast asleep.

A Bed for Hedgehog

Brown Bear lazed comfortably outside his den in the zoo, soaking up the soft rays of the autumn sun. He was thinking to himself, 'Very soon, when the cold weather really begins I shall move inside and doze during the day. Mmm, how nice!' And he stretched contentedly and smiled.

Suddenly, he felt something nudge his nose. He opened one eye and saw his friend Hedgehog.

'Hello Hedgehog,' he said. 'Enjoying the sun?'

'Well,' replied Hedgehog, 'I would be if I could feel it through these prickles of mine. The fact is, Brown Bear, I am feeling the cold dreadfully and I have nowhere to curl up for my winter sleep.'

'Why?' asked Brown Bear. 'Didn't the keeper put a pile of leaves in your house?'

'No,' replied Hedgehog mournfully, 'that's just the problem. He forgot all about me. So I decided to talk it over with you because you are so clever.'

'Thank you Hedgehog,' said Brown Bear proudly. 'Now, why don't you wander home while I think it over.'

Long after Hedgehog had gone, Brown Bear sat thinking and mumbling to himself. 'Pelican has a nice, big storage pouch under his bill, and Stork has a lovely long beak . . . and then there's Mouse and the Little Birds . . . they could help too . . .'

When he was satisfied with his plan, Brown Bear ambled off and gathered his friends together. Pelican, Stork, Mouse and the Little Birds all clustered around and listened to his plan, nodding wisely. Then they hurried away to start work, having agreed to meet Brown Bear at Hedgehog's house later on.

Pelican was the first to arrive, his pouch bulging with dry leaves; then Stork and the Little Birds with their beaks packed full; and finally Mouse, staggering under his load.

'Oh!' exclaimed Hedgehog, as he crawled in amongst the leaves. 'Are these for me? How kind!'

Brown Bear packed the leaves gently around Hedgehog and said in a quiet voice, 'Sleep well now Hedgehog and we'll see you in the spring.'

Stork in the Snow

Mother Stork was about to set off through the forest to find some food for herself and her little son, Sigmund.

'Be a good bird while I'm away, Sigmund!' she said.

Sigmund sat inside his cosy nest. It had been snowing in the forest, and Sigmund liked to peer over the edge of the nest at the white ground below.

'I think I'll fly down and have a *close* look at it,' he decided.

Sigmund couldn't fly well, and he fluttered down from his nest. He wandered about in the soft snow, really enjoying himself but, after a while, he began to feel cold, and he decided to go home. He flew up looking for his nest, but his wings were not strong enough to carry him far.

'Everything looks so different in the snow,' sobbed Sigmund. 'I don't know which tree my nest is in – *oh dear*!'

Now, Orlando Otter happened to pass by and heard Sigmund sobbing and sighing to himself.

'Are you lost, little stork?' he asked.

'I'm cold and I can't find my mummy!' sighed Sigmund.

'Then we must find her for you,' said Orlando. 'I expect she is flying about looking for you, at this very moment.'

Then Orlando had an idea. He picked up a stick, held it between his teeth, and began making marks in the snow. Clever Orlando was making a picture – a picture of Sigmund. With the stick, Orlando drew Sigmund's beak, his head, his body and his long, thin legs.

'The snow picture looks just like you, Sigmund,' said Orlando. 'Now, when Mother Stork flies overhead and sees the picture, she will know where you are.'

Meanwhile, Mother Stork had returned to her nest, and she was very worried when she could not find Sigmund. She flew here and there over the forest, looking for him. Suddenly, she saw Orlando's stork picture in the snow. She flew down at once, realising that Sigmund must be there. She was very pleased to see him, and thanked Orlando again and again for his clever drawing.

'Come along back to your nest now, Sigmund,' said Mother Stork. 'You must promise me not to wander off alone again until your wings are much stronger.' Sigmund promised, of course. Later, Mother Stork gave Orlando a tree-branch laden with his favourite juicy berries. It was the nicest present that Orlando could have had!

The Lonely Snail

The rain had stopped, so Sam the snail decided to go for a walk.

He glided up to a puddle and looked at his reflection in the water.

'Why is my shell such a dull brown colour?' he asked himself unhappily. 'I'd like to have a pretty yellow shell like those snails over there.' He looked towards a bed of nettles where a group of brightly coloured snails were enjoying their lunch. 'Nobody ever talks to me – I'm too dull and ugly.'

Suddenly, he heard a cry for help. Turning round he saw Tim, a baby snail, struggling in the water.

Tim had been playing at the edge of the puddle, but had fallen in as he tried to catch a floating leaf.

Sam hurried to the puddle and glided into the water. He reached Tim, and said, 'Climb on my back. We'll soon have you safe and dry.'

Tim sat on the big snail's shell and they soon reached the edge of the puddle.

'Now,' said Sam, 'tell me where you live, and I'll take you home.'

'My home's over there in the ivy,' answered Tim. 'Mummy told me not to go far, but I saw a butterfly and followed it here.'

Tim sat safely on Sam's shell and they set off for the ivy. Tim's Mummy was looking out anxiously and hurried to meet them.

Sam explained what had happened, and Mrs Snail led the way into her ivy house. 'I've just picked some tender young nettle leaves – do stay and have tea with us.'

When they had finished tea, Tim begged for another ride on his new friend's shell.

'You must come and see us again,' Mrs Snail said, as Sam prepared to go home.

Sam set off for home. He no longer felt sad or lonely.

'I don't mind being dull and brown now,' he said to himself. 'Now I can go and play with Tim and have tea with kind Mrs Snail whenever I like.'

And he made his way home feeling very proud and happy.

A Swim in the Rain

Gilbert the gosling lived in an orchard with lots of other goslings and adult geese. They all belonged to a boy named Timothy.

Every morning before going to school, Timothy went into the orchard to feed the geese.

As soon as Gilbert heard Timothy's voice, he went running to meet him, fluttering his little wings and wobbling along on his thin legs.

Sometimes Timothy would pick Gilbert up. He would stroke Gilbert's warm feathers and speak softly to him. Gilbert liked that very much and when he was put back on the ground again, he would run along behind Timothy making funny little noises.

One morning, after Timothy had shut the gate and gone off to school, Gilbert thought he would go down to the stream at the bottom of the orchard.

When he got there he found the stream empty. There had been so much sunshine and so little rain in past weeks that all the water had dried up.

Poor Gilbert felt very unhappy. He wanted to paddle in the cool water. Never mind, he would go and look for water somewhere else. Perhaps he could find another stream, or a pond or even a large puddle.

Gilbert walked up to the top of the orchard, where he saw a big toad. He thought that if he could follow the toad it might lead him to some water.

But the toad leaped along so fast and so high that Gilbert's little legs could not keep up with him and soon the toad disappeared from sight.

Sadly, he walked along the top of the orchard and started down the other side, but he could not see any water.

Soon poor Gilbert began to feel cold. The wind was blowing now and when he looked up at the sky he saw that the sun had gone in and there were lots of dark clouds.

He started to run back quickly towards his house, where he knew all the other geese would be. When he was almost there, it began to rain.

Gilbert was so happy now that he did not want to go home. Instead, he turned round and went to the bottom of the orchard again.

This time there was a little water in the stream. Gilbert tumbled in and splashed about in the muddy water. It was raining hard now and the water was getting deeper and deeper all the time.

Quite soon Gilbert was swimming. First he swam up the stream and then he turned round and swam back downstream. He was enjoying himself.

The rain stopped after a few minutes. The sun began to shine, the wind dropped and the sky was blue again.

Gilbert's feathers soon dried in the sun and he was just thinking he should go home, when he heard Timothy calling his name.

Timothy had been looking for Gilbert since he got home from school, so he was very pleased to see the little gosling climbing out of the stream. Timothy picked him up and carried him back to his house, where all the other geese were waiting for him.

Timothy said goodnight and shut Gilbert safely inside his house for the night. Gilbert snuggled down happily beside another little gosling and, a moment later, fell fast asleep.

Miss Mouse
has a Visitor

Miss Brenda Mouse was making a cake. She had put the butter and sugar into a large red bowl and she was putting in the flour, when there was a *rat-a-tat-tat* at the door.

'Just a minute,' she cried, as she ran to wash her paws.

Rat-a-tat-tat.

'I'm coming,' cried Miss Mouse, as she dried her paws on a big, blue towel.

Rat-a-tat-tat.

She opened the door. She looked to the left. She looked to the right. But there was no-one to be seen. She closed the door.

Rat-a-tat-tat.

She opened the door. She looked to the left. She looked to the right. But she couldn't see anyone.

'I'm down here,' said a little voice.

Miss Mouse looked down and saw a funny little green creature with a green, furry tail and a big, green nose. It was dressed in a yellow top hat and a smart yellow and blue suit. In its little green hand it held a suitcase.

'Good morning,' it said, raising its yellow top hat. 'I am a Wiggin and I am looking for a home. I have come a long way,' said the little green thing. 'Are there any homes for sale here?'

'I do not know,' said Miss Mouse. But my friend, Mr Rudolph Rat, may know of a home for sale. He lives in the dustbin across the yard. My name is Miss Brenda Mouse.'

They went across the yard to the dustbin and knocked on the door.

Mr Rudolph Rat opened the door.

'Good morning, Mr Rudolph. This is Mr Wiggin and he is looking for a home.'

'Let me think,' said Mr Rudolph. 'The old boot next to Miss Kitten's home is empty.'

The three of them went across the yard to look at the boot.

'Oh, it is a perfect home,' cried Mr Wiggin. 'Thank you. You must both come to tea tomorrow.'

'We should like that. Thank you,' said Miss Mouse and Mr Rudolph.

'Now I must go back to my cake,' said Miss Mouse. 'I'll bring you some to-morrow,' she called to her new friend as she left.

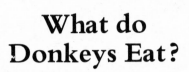

What do Donkeys Eat?

The twins, Tim and Tessa, were delighted when Dad bought them a donkey for their birthday.

'Where shall we keep her?' they asked.

'In the back orchard,' said Dad. 'She can eat the grass.'

So the donkey, which they named Dandy, went to live in the back orchard, with a little shed to shelter in when it rained.

She ate other things as well as grass. She ate the leaves and twigs from the apple-trees, and any apples that she could reach. She ate brambles and blackberries from the hedge. There were some tall thistles growing in the orchard, and she ate those. One day Mummy put a tea-cloth to dry, over the orchard gate, and Dandy ate that, too.

'I'm sure she must be hungry,' said Tania, the twin's big sister.

'Nonsense,' said Dad. 'You're always giving her bread and scraps, besides her breakfast of hay every morning, and all that grass she eats.'

'I don't think she gets the right sort of food,' said Tania. 'I'll borrow a book from the library, to see what she ought to eat.'

So she brought home a library book, with the title, *How to Care for Donkeys*.

In the book there were some coloured pictures of donkeys, and Tania thought that Dandy might like them. So, when she went out to give Dandy some crusts after tea, she took the book with her.

But Dandy was nowhere to be seen. She had disappeared.

'Oh dear!' thought Tania. 'She has eaten her way through the hedge and escaped.'

She went hurrying off to the far end of the orchard, leaving her book on Dandy's feeding-trough.

But Dandy had not escaped – she was only hiding behind her little shed. She soon came out to see what Tania had brought for her. When she saw the book on the trough, she started to eat it!

Presently, Tania came hurrying back.

'Oh, you wicked little animal!' she exclaimed. 'You've ruined the book!'

And so she had. She had taken several big bites out of the pages.

'Now we shall never know what donkeys eat,' said Mummy.

'Oh yes we shall,' laughed Dad. 'They eat library books!'

The Farmer's Son

Once upon a time, there lived a farmer and his wife. They were very happy together. But one thing was wrong – no son had been born to them.

Every evening, the farmer would lean on his plough, and say, 'I wish I had a son to plough my fields. If only he would fall out of the sky!'

Then, one evening, while the farmer was saying this, a hawk flew overhead carrying a little mouse in his claws. The hawk dropped the mouse and it fell right in front of the farmer.

The farmer picked up the little mouse, and said 'Where did you come from?'

'The sky, sir,' said the mouse.

'Then you must be my son,' said the farmer to the mouse. 'Will you come home with me and plough my fields?'

'Of course, sir,' said the mouse.

So the farmer took the mouse home.

Now the mouse was very good at ploughing, and the farmer and his wife grew to love their little son very much.

But as the years went by, the little mouse seemed to grow sad and the farmer and his wife were very worried about him.

Then, one day, the farmer's wife took out her tape-measure and measured her son. 'I know what is the matter with our son. He is a fully grown mouse now and he needs a wife.'

'We must find him a worthy wife,' said the farmer.

The farmer and the little mouse set out the next day to find a bride for the mouse. But they searched all day long in vain. Sadly, they both sat down on a rock and looked up at the sky.

Suddenly, the farmer cried, 'Look how beautiful the Moon is, son. Would you like her for your bride?'

'She is very beautiful,' he said. 'But she is too cold and proud.'

'You are right,' said the Moon. 'I am not for you.'

Then the farmer said, 'Is there no-one better than you?'

'Yes,' said the Moon. 'The Cloud is. She can hide my face completely.' Just then, a cloud slipped over the moon.

'Look, son,' said the farmer. 'That is the wife for you.'

'But she is so gloomy,' said the mouse.

'You are right,' said the Cloud. 'I am not for you.'

'Is there no-one better than you?' the farmer asked the Cloud.

'Yes,' said the Cloud. 'The Wind. She can blow me wherever she wishes.' Just then, the Wind blew the cloud away.

'There is a good strong wife for you,' said the farmer to his son.

'She is not for me,' shivered the mouse. 'She fidgets too much.'

'Yes, I am restless,' said the Wind. 'I am not for you.'.

'Is there no-one better than you?' the farmer asked the Wind.

'Yes,' replied the Wind. 'The Mountain. I cannot move her, however hard I blow.'

The farmer turned round and saw that they were sitting at the base of a high mountain. 'Now we have found you a wife, son,' said the farmer.

'But she is far too stubborn,' said the little mouse.

'Yes,' boomed the Mountain. 'I am not for you. I will not budge.'

Then the farmer said, 'Tell me, Mountain, is there no-one better than you?'

'Yes, there is,' said the Mountain. 'There is someone who is digging little holes inside me and will one day destroy me. Dig into my side and you will find her.'

So the farmer and his son each took a shovel and began to dig and dig and dig. Suddenly, a great hole appeared in front of the farmer and his son and out stepped a pretty lady-mouse!

The farmer's son held out his hand to the lady mouse and they walked slowly home together.

The Happy Reindeer

Many, many years ago, there was a beautiful little fawn named Bo. He lived in a cold country where the snow lay thick and deep each winter.

Now, Bo was a very gentle reindeer. He liked nothing better than to play with the little children when they came out of school at the end of the day.

As the days and months went by, Bo grew into a handsome creature, with a beautiful set of antlers. But even though he looked big and strong, he remained gentle and loving. Whenever he was missing, his mother always knew where

to find him. He would be waiting outside the village school in the valley. When the children came out they would skip by his side and race him to the pond, where they would slide on the ice together.

'It is strange,' his mother would say, 'Bo seems to enjoy playing with children rather than his own reindeer friends.'

Then one day, just before Christmas, a man dressed in a red coat came to the little village. He had a beard as white as snow. He seemed to be searching for something, but no-one knew what. Then quite suddenly he saw Bo surrounded by a group of children.

'Ah!' said the delighted stranger, 'there's the reindeer I am looking for.' And without waiting another moment, the stranger went over and patted Bo.

'As you are so fond of children,' said the old man, 'I have a very special job for you, and one that I am sure you will enjoy.' So Bo followed the old man to a grotto, and inside there were piles and piles of beautiful toys. The old man filled several sacks with the toys, then he gave Bo a sack of his favourite food – lichen plants.

'Now, Bo,' said the old man kindly, 'will you pull my sleigh for me?' Bo was soon trotting over the crisp snow with Santa Claus, to deliver toys to all the children, who were fast asleep in their beds.

It was a beautiful night and Bo was the happiest reindeer in the whole world. Some people say that he was the very first reindeer to help Santa Claus on his Christmas travels.

A Boat-Trip to See the Puffins

In the summer holidays, Mark went to stay with his Uncle John who lived in Scotland near the coast.

'Come on Mark,' said Uncle John one morning. 'Let's go down and look at the beach.'

Mark felt a little disappointed when they arrived at the sea. The coastline was very rocky right down to the beach, and there wasn't much sand. And soon it began to rain.

'We often have rain here,' said Uncle John, smiling at Mark's unhappy face. 'But we have something else right here on the beach – my rowing boat. Coming for a trip along the coast?'

The boat was high on the beach. She was painted yellow and her name was *Sea-Bird*.

Mark cheered up straight away as they pushed the boat out on to the water.

Uncle John rowed out a little way and Mark could see further along the coast with its bays and rocks, lined by the foamy tide. A lot of gulls were circling and screaming above them.

'Now, look over there, with my binoculars,' said Uncle John, pointing at a rocky inlet. 'What can you see?'

Mark peered through the binoculars. He could see birds with big, bright red and grey beaks, walking about on the shore.

'They look like parrots,' he said excitedly.

'They are puffins', said his uncle. 'Sometimes they're called sea-parrots. Comical fellows, aren't they?'

'They've got orange legs,' laughed Mark. 'Oh look – there's one flying!' He stood up with the binoculars and the boat rocked violently. 'Hey! Sit down', said Uncle John, pulling him by his coat. 'I don't want to see you – or my binoculars – in the sea!'

'His legs were dangling when he flew,' said Mark. 'He is a funny bird. I wonder where he's flying to.'

'He's probably looking for fish,' said Uncle John. 'They dive and catch a lot of fish in their big beaks. They like fish and shrimps.'

'So do I,' said Mark 'I've never seen puffins before.'

'They only live on wild coasts like this,' said his uncle. 'They dig out burrows for their nests then lay just one egg.'

'They're fun,' chuckled Mark. 'They look like little clowns strutting about with their painted beaks. I'm glad we came. Can we go and look for something interesting again tomorrow?'

The Fox Who Ate Too Much

Once upon a time, there lived a fox named Roberto, who was very greedy. He was also lazy and refused to work, so he used to steal his food.

He ate the corn that was thrown out for the ducks, drank the cats' milk, ate the dogs' dinners and took any food that the villagers had left unguarded in their houses.

One day, Leander Muffit had just finished making some pancakes, when she heard the front doorbell ring. She left the hot pancakes on a dish and went to answer the door. But there was nobody there!

Roberto had rung the doorbell and run round to the back of the house. He slipped in through the open back door and stole all of Leander's pancakes.

When Leander was back in the kitchen, she saw Roberto Fox hurrying away with all her pancakes. Leander was very angry indeed. The next day, she called a secret meeting of all her neighbours and told them of a plan she had to outwit Roberto. They all thought it was a very good idea.

Later that week, Roberto was snooping in Mrs Creamery's garden, when he smelt cream cakes. So he put his paw through the open kitchen window and grabbed several cream buns. As he ate the buns, he decided that something was wrong. 'They taste horrid,' he thought.

He decided to move on to Mrs Hubbard's house. Lying on the table was some delicious-looking fudge. Roberto waited until Mrs Hubbard was out of the kitchen, and then he ate the fudge in three gulps! It tasted even nastier than the cream buns.

He went to another house, but the same thing happened there, and at the next house, and the next, until he felt so ill and had such a pain that he thought he would never eat again.

Everyone in the village had baked something specially for Roberto Fox to steal. But they had put pepper, or salt, or mustard, or vinegar in the food!

No-one heard or saw Roberto for the next few days. He was lying at home feeling very ill and very sorry for himself.

While Roberto was lying in bed, he did some thinking. 'I have never had any real friends,' he said to himself, 'and now everyone has played a trick on me.' After a while, he realized that it was all his fault that he had no friends, so he decided to mend his ways and never be greedy or lazy or to steal from anyone again.

When Roberto was better, he went back to the village and asked everyone to forgive him for his bad ways. The villagers were kind and forgave him.

When Roberto went to see Leander, she asked, 'What work are you going to do now, Roberto?'

'I don't know,' replied the fox.

Leander felt sorry for poor Roberto, so she said, 'You can work for me and help me bake my cakes.'

'Thank you, Leander,' said Roberto. 'I am very grateful.' And so he was. From that day to this, Roberto has never stolen anything or eaten any of Leander's cakes without asking her first.

Now Roberto and Leander are the very best of friends.

Glossy the Hero

Glossy the starling was having his breakfast in bed, because he had worked so hard scouting for food and guarding the young starlings.

'Bon! Bon! Come back at once! Bon! Bon!' he heard his mother calling.

Glossy wondered sleepily what his youngest brother was up to. Baby Bon had just learned to fly but only to the first branch below the nest.

'Bon! Glossy! Father! Come here – quick, quick!'

Other starlings from nearby nests were also calling out.

Something was wrong, thought Glossy. How could his mother have forgotten that his father was on a long scout for the day otherwise? His brothers, too, had all gone to work. Of course! He remembered then – *he* was the one in charge!

Wide-awake at last, Glossy hopped to the top of the nest. He had completely forgotten about his special treat of breakfast in bed! He soon saw what had happened.

Baby Bon had flown further than usual and he had had to rest on the roof of a shed below their tree. He was too frightened to try and fly back to the nest.

Just ready to spring on poor Baby Bon was a big, black, angry-looking cat!

'Bon! Bon!' called Mother Starling and all her friends.

Glossy swooped down, swerving between Bon and the big, black cat.

The cat hissed angrily and turned his head to glare with pale green eyes at Glossy.

The noise from the tree grew louder and louder. 'Now, *up* Bon! Fly up! Up! Up!' chorused the starlings.

Glossy had an idea. He dropped one wing as if he had hurt it and dragged it on the roof. Then he hopped a little way towards the edge.

The cat got ready to spring again. This time he was after Glossy.

'Up, Bon! Up!' called the starlings again.

Glossy hopped across the roof and flipped over the edge just in time. The cat's four paws came down with a bang on the roof. Then Glossy heard the glad cry of the other starlings.

'He's done it! Bon's done it! He's quite safe now!'

Then every starling in the tree shouted to Glossy, 'Quick! Quick!'

There was no need to tell Glossy twice. He flew up into the air as the cat sprang forward. The cat fell off the shed and on to the lawn below. He rolled over and shook himself. He was very, very angry.

But Glossy was back in the nest with his mother and Baby Bon. And all the other mother starlings gathered round to tell him how wonderful he was.

'Oh, Glossy, how brave you are! You are a hero!'

And then his mother said in her softest voice, 'Glossy, I'm so *proud* of you, my clever son!'

There is another story about Glossy the starling on page 42.

Ben's Special Day

'Orders to deliver one raccoon to a Mr McIntosh at the Green Trees Wildlife Park,' announced the driver of a truck at the Main Gates.

The gates opened with a clang and the truck drove between tall trees to the Office. There it stopped, and the driver took a heavy basket out of the back

paws in the water and wishing he had some crayfish to eat. Crayfish was his favourite food! It was very pleasant there by the stream and he felt far too shy to meet the giraffe or the bear or the goat or any of the other animals for that matter.

Here he is, Mr McIntosh. All bright-eyed and bushy-tailed! It's a special day for the little fellow, starting out on holiday from the big City Zoo, and he's only a few months old. Oh, and by the way,' he called as he started up his truck, 'he answers to the name of Ben.'

'Well then,' said Mr McIntosh to Ben, who felt very shy and a little afraid, 'you're the finest little raccoon I've seen.' And he showed Ben to his daughter Phoebe. She was ten years old and she liked him at once.

'Come along Ben,' said Phoebe as she carried the basket into the Animal Nursery enclosure. 'You'll like it here with all the other young animals.'

She put the basket down by a little stream and then she left him alone. Ben climbed out and sat very quietly in the reeds, dipping his

'Hello,' said a croaky voice. It was a large toad. 'Must be quite a special day for you,' he said. 'First day on holiday and lots of new friends to make . . .'

'Yes . . . well . . . I thought I might spend today here in the reeds, out of their way,' replied Ben shyly.

'Impossible!' declared the toad. 'No chance of hiding now—Phoebe's due in a few minutes. She comes in here to read her book every afternoon and give us each something tasty to eat. Now, today's Wednesday, so she'll have fresh mackerel for Queenie the penguin, juicy leaves for Jasmine the giraffe, honey for Bruce the bear and, I dare say, a

little bit ot crayfish for you! How does that sound?'

'Delicious,' sighed Ben, 'but I haven't the courage to go out and meet all those other animals.'

'Oh, you won't have to,' croaked the toad. 'Phoebe will come to you.'

It wasn't long before Phoebe found him. She picked him up, carried him over to her reading chair and sat him down at her feet. Then she gave him a big, tasty piece of crayfish and began to read a story in a soft, clear voice. And do you know what the title

of that story was? BEN'S SPECIAL DAY!

It all seemed like a dream to Ben. He closed his eyes and listened to Phoebe and forgot his shyness. Then he felt a sharp little tug at his tail and, looking around, he saw all the animals clustered about him. Among them was a hedgehog. 'Mind if I sit on your tail to listen, Ben?' he asked. 'More comfortable than the ground.'

Ben said, 'No, of course not.' He was pleased and, with thoughts of holidays and crayfish and friends, he settled down again, a little closer to Phoebe this time.

Learning About Animal Patterns

Daddy took the twins, Edward and Emma, to the zoo for a birthday treat. Edward took his camera with him and Emma wore her pretty new pink dress.

'Aren't there a lot of patterned animals?' said Emma, after they had looked at the striped zebra, spotted leopard and splodgy giraffe.

'Their markings can help to protect them,' explained Daddy. 'If an animal is the same colour or pattern as its surroundings it can't be seen so easily by a stronger animal or hunter wanting to catch it. A polar-bear is well hidden against white snow . . .'

'. . . Or a brown frog in the mud,' suggested Emma.

'. . . Or a striped tiger – its stripes look a bit like blades of grass,' said Edward.

'That's right,' said Daddy. 'And the markings on the giraffe and leopard make them well-hidden amongst leaves when the sun shines through them. The sun makes everything else look dappled as well.'

'What's the animal which changes colour?' asked Edward.

'That's the chameleon,' said Daddy. 'He moves very slowly and if he were seen he would be caught easily. So, he can actually change from brown to green if he wants to sit on a rock or walk in the grass.'

'That's clever,' said Edward, and he took some photographs of patterned animals because they were so interesting.

The children had a lovely day at the zoo, but all too soon it was time to go home.

'Can I just take a photo of the flamingoes?' said Edward. 'They're such a lovely colour.' The flamingoes were bright pink birds with long necks, curved beaks and long thin legs, and they were standing in some shallow water.

Daddy and Emma stood near them to have their photograph taken before they went home. 'I can't see Emma properly,' said Edward, puzzled, as he looked through his camera. 'I can only see you, Daddy. Where's Emma?'

'I'm here!' laughed Emma, waving her hand. Edward looked again. 'So you are,' he said. 'For a minute, I thought you'd disappeared.'

'It's because Emma's dress is the same colour as the flamingoes,' said Daddy. 'Camouflage again, you see!'

Emma thought the flamingoes were the most beautiful birds she had ever seen. She picked up a soft curling pink feather from the ground, to take home and remind her of them.

Jumping Kangaroos

Karrington Kangaroo was bouncing about like a rubber ball.

'Whatever is Karrington trying to do?' wondered Kinder, his little brother. 'Hey! Be careful!' he snorted, as Karrington bounded right over his head.

He took shelter behind a gum tree and watched as Karrington *bounced* and *bounced* and *bounced*.

'He must have eaten something odd,' sighed Kinder, as Karrington sailed over a bush twice as high as himself.

'Hey! Stop a minute, Karrington!' he called, catching hold of Karrington's tail to keep him still.

'What is it?' asked Karrington. 'Can't you see I'm busy?'

'But busy doing what?' asked Kinder.

'Jumping,' said Karrington, anxious to be off. 'Let go of my tail.'

'Not until you tell me what you are doing,' said Kinder, and he sat on Karrington's tail.

'Have you heard about that cow who jumped over the moon?' asked Karrington impatiently.

'Yes,' said Kinder. 'Of course I've heard that nursery rhyme.'

'Well,' said Karrington, with a toss of his head, 'if a cow can jump over the moon then so can a kangaroo. And I'm going to be the first to do it.'

That made Kinder think. Anything a cow could do, a kangaroo could do just as well, if not better.

'I think I'll join you,' he said.

'Good!' laughed Karrington. 'The more the merrier.'

So if you ever see kangaroos jumping and bouncing about like rubber balls, you will know what they are trying to do. But it's a big jump to the moon.

103

Bimbo Meets a Friendly Badger

Bimbo the budgerigar was on his way home to Amanda after his visit to the farm when, suddenly, he changed his mind and skimmed over the fields to the wood.

At the edge of the wood he stopped to rest on a fence. Frisking about in the grass was a young rabbit with a pink nose and big ears.

'I've never seen a bird like you before,' he said, twitching his nose.

'I'm just here on a visit,' replied Bimbo.

'Come and meet Badger then,' said the rabbit, hopping off.

By the time they reached Badger's place, Bimbo was feeling very tired.

'You look as if you've had enough visiting for one day,' said Badger kindly.

'Yes, I *am* tired,' agreed Bimbo, 'and I'll never be able to fly home tonight.'

'Well then, you must spend the night in the wood,' said Badger. 'Come on, we'll go and see Squirrel and he'll find you a nice, cosy bed.'

So they went off together to look for Squirrel just as the sun was setting behind the trees.

Read about Bimbo the budgerigar's night in the wood on page 156.

The Beautiful Squirrel

Anna was the most beautiful squirrel in the wood. Her coat was so red and her tail so bushy, that she made all the other animals look quite dull. But she was also very proud and, because of this, she had no real friends.

One day in spring, Mr Cyril Squirrel, who lived on the far side of the wood, called upon Anna to ask her to be his bride. But Anna laughed, and replied, 'Why, when I marry, I shall expect to become Queen of the Woods, or at least a Princess.'

Cyril went sadly away, but very soon forgot Anna and married another pretty squirrel.

Anna became more and more unhappy because no one seemed to notice her anymore. Everyone was much too busy taking care of babies, or gathering acorns for the winter.

One day, when Anna sat gazing at herself in a puddle, Mrs Bunny's four cheeky children peeped out of their burrow to giggle at her, and at that moment a robin flew down from a hawthorn bush and perched on her tail.

'What a silly girl you are, Anna,' chirped the robin. 'Why, my feathers are much brighter than your fur, but I am not proud like you.' Then he flew away before Anna could reply.

Anna scampered quickly back to her tree home and there she began to cry. 'The robin is right,' she thought. 'I am vain and silly to think that I would be loved for my beauty alone.'

Early next morning, when she was gathering some nuts, Anna met many little animals busy with their tasks around the wood, and for each one she had a smile and a cheery word. Everyone was very surprised.

Later that day, Mrs Hare brought Anna an invitation to the woodland autumn party. That night, Anna really looked her best.

Everyone admired Anna's red fur, but she pretended not to notice. Instead, she told the other animals how nice *they* were looking and how happy she was to be there.

During the evening, Cyril brought his brother to meet her. He was a very handsome squirrel. Anna and Cyril's brother met many times after that and in the spring they were married. It was a very happy day and a special guest at the wedding was Anna's new friend, the wise little robin.

A New Life for the Roundabout Horse

Prancer was a very dashing roundabout horse with grey and black dapple markings. But, he was always grumbling.

'I'm fed up with going round and round all day,' he moaned. 'I want to see something of the world.'

But Prancer was not the only one feeling grumpy that night. Not far away in a stable, another dappled horse called Henry was also grumbling.

'This caravan gets heavier every day. I would give anything to be like those roundabout horses.'

Now it so happened that a fairy was passing and decided to teach the discontented pair a lesson. She waved her wand and in a flash Prancer was in Henry's stable, while Henry was in Prancer's place on the roundabout.

The next day, Prancer was harnessed up to the caravan and set off at a steady trit-trot, eager to see the world. After a while his legs began to ache and his hooves began to go slower and slower till his new owner was very cross with him.

Meanwhile, Henry was finding that a life of rest on a roundabout was not so pleasant after all. Going round and round made his poor head spin.

That night the fairy called Prancer and Henry to her and asked them how they were enjoying their new lives. The two horses looked at each other and in one voice they begged to be allowed to return to their proper places.

The fairy smiled. 'It shall be done,' she said, and in a flash they were both back home.

'It's good to be back,' sighed Henry to his companions. 'You know I shall be really glad to get out with that caravan again tomorrow.'

Back at the roundabout the other horses asked, 'And how was the outside world?'

Prancer smiled. 'All I want to see of the world is right here.'

The Cat
Who was Too Proud

Once there was a sleek and beautiful cat called Mr Moggett. His fur was as black as night and his eyes were the colour of buttercups. He was also very proud, and he was sure there was not another cat like him in the whole world. Old Mrs Tabby, whose ears were tattered and whose stripes were higgledy-piggledy, told him not to be silly, that there were dozens of cats like him.

'Nonsense!' he would say. 'There can't possibly be.'

'Mark my words,' said old Mrs Tabby. 'One of these days you will have a nasty surprise.'

Mr Moggett didn't believe that either.

Then one day, when Mr Moggett and Mrs Tabby were sitting on the front porch, a man riding a big penny-farthing bicycle came past the gate. He was wearing a big top hat and he was calling through a megaphone,

'Come to the fair . . .'

He was followed by a procession of lorries and caravans, all with the words 'Alfred's Fair' written on them in big red letters.

'Miaow!' said Mrs Tabby. 'How exciting! I *do* like going to the fair.'

'How quaint!' said Mr Moggett, who had never been to a fair in his life.

'Why don't you come along too?' asked Mrs Tabby.

'I will if you insist,' said Mr Moggett grandly. 'But not for long,' he added.

That afternoon when the lorries had been unloaded, the big dipper had been put up and the big organ on the round-about was humming with a gay, jangly tune, Mr Moggett and Mrs Tabby went to the fair. All the people in the village seemed to be there and no-one noticed the two cats as they slipped through the main gate.

Mr Moggett looked up at the big dipper.

'I shan't go on that,' he said.

'Of course not,' said Mrs Tabby. 'I only come to watch. I don't go whirling about on things like that.'

They were watching a man throwing balls at coconuts when it began to rain. Mr Moggett ran to the nearest tent.

'We'll go in there,' he said. 'I don't want to get my fur wet.'

'I . . . I don't think you will like it in there,' said Mrs Tabby, who knew what was inside the tent.

'Yes I will,' replied Mr Moggett as he disappeared inside. Mrs Tabby hurried after him. She found him inside the big tent, staring in astonishment at a black cat, who was just as beautiful, and just as surprised as himself.

'If I hadn't seen it with my own eyes I wouldn't have believed it,' gasped Mr Moggett. 'How dare there be another cat like myself.' He hissed at the strange cat, and the strange cat hissed at him.

'Come away,' pleaded Mrs Tabby.

'I will not,' said Mr Moggett, and with his nose in the air he pushed his way past her and into the middle of the tent. He could hardly believe his eyes. The tent was full of beautiful black cats, all with bright yellow eyes, and all staring at him. He drew himself up haughtily, arched

his back and hissed at them. And all the other beautiful black cats arched their backs and hissed back at him.

Poor Mr Moggett was so overcome that he ran all the way home and sat miserably in front of the fire.

A long time afterwards, Mrs Tabby came home. She didn't tell Mr Moggett that he had been in the hall of mirrors, and that all the cats he had seen were simply reflections of himself. That was a secret he must never know.

Henry Hare
Cures his Hiccups

'Good gracious!' exclaimed Jenny Rabbit. 'That's the sixth time you've hiccupped this morning.'

'I know,' said Henry Hare miserably, 'but I just can't stop. Can you help me, Jenny?'

'Well,' said Jenny thoughtfully, 'someone told me once that if you can hold your breath, you will stop hiccupping. Shall we try?'

Poor Henry said he would try anything to get rid of them.

'Now hold your breath until I count to ten,' said Jenny. Henry took a deep breath and Jenny started to count, 'One, two, three, four . . .' But before she could count to five, Henry gave another loud hiccup.

'Oh dear, that's no good,' he sighed.

'Shall we try drinking water? That might help,' said Jenny, and off they went to a nearby pond.

As soon as Henry had drunk the water he started hiccupping again.

'Oh dear, it's no use. I'll never get rid of them,' he said.

Just then Benny Badger appeared.

'Hello, you two,' he said. 'What's the matter, Henry?'

'I've got hiccups. Can you help me, Benny?' asked Henry.

Benny sat down and thought for a while, then he said, 'Yes indeed, I do know how to cure hiccups. Pass that jam jar, Jenny.'

'Now, Henry,' said Benny, holding the jar in front of Henry's face. 'I want you to catch the next four hiccups in this jar.'

Just at that moment Henry gave a loud hiccup.

'Good,' said Benny. 'Only three more.'

They did not have to wait long – soon Henry had caught all four hiccups.

Benny covered the jar with a big leaf, and gave it a good shake.

'What are you doing?' asked Jenny.

'Well, if I shake the jar long enough the hiccups will join together into one big one,' explained Benny, 'and then I can throw the jar into the pond.'

He shook the jar and with a big heave he threw it into the centre of the pond.

'There go your hiccups, Henry. They won't come back,' chuckled Benny.

A Friend
for Porcupine

A porcupine wandered alone through a forest.

'I'm always alone!' sighed the porcupine to himself. 'I need a friend.'

He met a chipmunk, and asked the chipmunk to be his friend. The chipmunk looked at his long quills.

'No,' said the chipmunk. 'You are too prickly to be my friend. You might hurt me.'

The porcupine walked on, and soon he met a bear. He asked the bear to be his friend.

'No,' said the bear, 'you are too prickly to be my friend. You might hurt me.'

The porcupine walked on, and soon he met a beaver. He asked the beaver to be his friend.

'No,' said the beaver, 'you are too prickly to be my friend. You might hurt me.'

The sad porcupine wandered to the end of the forest, and he came, at last, to a beach. There, the porcupine met a turtle.

'Cheer up, Porcupine,' said the turtle. 'You look sad.'

'The chipmunk won't be my friend,' explained the porcupine. 'The bear won't be my friend. The beaver won't be my friend, either. They say I'm too prickly. I know I'm a prickly fellow, but I'm also lonely. It's no use asking you to be my friend, is it? You'll say I'm too prickly, as the others did.'

To the porcupine's surprise, the turtle replied, 'I will be your friend. I don't mind prickles at all. You see, I have a hard shell to protect me from your prickles. We'll meet every day and go for walks and chat together. That's what friends do you know.'

'I've found a friend! I've found a friend!' the porcupine thought happily to himself, as he walked slowly along the beach with the turtle. 'No more lonely days for me!'

Cake for the Birds

Fairy Buttercup was very busy in her kitchen. She was making a Fly-Away Surprise Cake for Fairy Cowslip's birthday. Cowslip was her best friend.

When the mixture was ready, she poured it into a round tin and popped it into the hot oven. It was not long before the cake was cooked. Buttercup lifted it carefully out of the oven, and left it to cool by the open window.

Outside in the garden the birds were having a meeting.

'We're hungry, Wise Owl,' complained the pigeon. 'It's been such a hot summer that there's nothing much to eat, and we don't know what to do.'

All the birds looked at Wise Owl, waiting for him to say something. He fluffed his feathers and said, 'Yes, now . . . there must be a way to . . .' The birds watched as a dreamy smile spread over Wise Owl's face.

'Well, go on,' prompted Sparrow.

'There's the most delicious smell coming from Fairy Buttercup's kitchen . . .' replied Wise Owl vaguely.

'What good is that to us?' snapped the sparrow.

'Don't get cross, Sparrow,' answered Wise Owl. 'I have been told that Buttercup is a rather good cook. She may have made something for us to eat. Why don't you call in at the window and ask her, Robin.'

Robin could hardly believe his eyes when he saw the cake on Buttercup's window-sill. 'Oh Buttercup!' he chirped. 'How sweet of you to make us all such a beautiful cake!'

'W-What . . .' began Fairy Buttercup, looking astonished.

'Perhaps you could put it outside on the grass for us. Then we wouldn't get in your way.'

Too surprised to say anything, Buttercup carried the cake out to the garden.

Birds came flying from everywhere, all chattering at once. Buttercup stood at the door and watched miserably as they gobbled up her lovely cake.

Then, suddenly, she burst out laughing. 'No wonder it was called a Fly-Away Cake,' she chuckled. And she went inside to bake another one.

Lassie's Long Walk

Once there was a little puppy named Lassie. She had short, wobbly legs, soft brown eyes and a very waggy tail.

Lassie lived in a big house with her little master, Jeremy.

One day, Jeremy's Mummy told him that Lassie could go with them to the woods for a walk.

When they reached the woods, Mummy sat down on the grass while Lassie and Jeremy played in the leaves, until they were both feeling tired. Then Mummy said she would read a book to Jeremy and so he sat down beside her. Lassie was busy sniffing and scratching around the trees.

When Mummy had finished reading, Jeremy got up to look for Lassie, but he couldn't find her anywhere. Jeremy and Mummy called and called her, but she did not come.

Lassie had walked through the woods and out into a field. She was too far away to hear Mummy and Jeremy calling her.

Suddenly, she heard a loud mooing sound. She looked through the hedge and saw a cow. 'Hello, cow,' said Lassie. 'I am lost. Please can you help me find my master?' The cow said she was sorry but she could not, because the farmer would be coming at any moment to take her back to the cowshed for milking. So Lassie said good-bye to the cow.

Next, Lassie met a big, fluffy rabbit. He was sitting in the sunshine, washing his ears and his whiskers. 'Hello, rabbit,' said Lassie. 'I am lost. Please can you help me find my master?' The rabbit said he would try. He put his big ear to the ground and listened. Then he told Lassie that he could hear her master, a long way away, in the woods. Lassie thanked the rabbit and said good-bye. She was wondering which path to follow when she saw a blackbird sitting on a tree-stump.

'Hello, blackbird,' said Lassie. 'I am lost. Please can you help me find my master. He is in the woods somewhere.'

The blackbird said he had seen Lassie's master, just round the next corner and that he would fly in front and show her the way.

They had just turned the corner, when Lassie saw Jeremy and Mummy. She ran up to them, crying and wagging her tail. Jeremy was very pleased to see her. He hugged and patted her and told her how worried he had been.

Mummy could see that the little puppy was very, very tired, so she carried her all the way home in her shopping-basket.

As soon as they arrived home, Mummy put some warm milk into Lassie's dish. Lassie was very pleased and wagged her tail all the time she was drinking.

When she had finished her drink, Jeremy carried her into the lounge and sat down on the carpet beside her. Lassie was sorry she had gone off all by herself. She put her head on Jeremy's lap and fell fast asleep.

The Little Speckled Hen

It was quite the nicest cottage in the village, and inside lived old Mrs Flummage. In the henhouse at the bottom of the garden she kept a little speckled hen.

Now Mrs Flummage's garden was very small, so the little speckled hen's pen had to be very small too.

'Poor little speckled hen,' said Mrs Flummage.

Then one morning she had a bright idea. 'I will let you go out on to the village green,' she said. 'Then, this evening, I will fetch you and shut you up in the henhouse as usual, to keep you safe from foxes.'

The little speckled hen enjoyed herself all day on the village green.

Then at last the sun began to go down, so Mrs Flummage came out and called, 'Come along! Come along!' But the little speckled hen refused.

Mrs Flummage started to chase the little speckled hen, but the little speckled hen clucked, 'You will never catch me!'

Round and round the village green went the little speckled hen, and round and round after her went Mrs Flummage.

'Oh, let *me* catch her for you,' called Mr Jockle-Wockle, who lived in the house next door.

'Please do,' puffed Mrs Flummage.

So round the village green ran Mr Jockle-Wockle, and round and round went the little speckled hen. Not even he could catch her!

Suddenly Mrs Flummage had an idea. 'We will find some friends, and we will all chase the little speckled hen together,' she said.

So they called on some more neighbours, and round the village green they ran, and round went the little speckled hen.

This time they were too quick for the little speckled hen. 'Caught you!' cried Mrs Flummage, picking her up.

The little speckled hen was allowed out on the village green again in the morning, but when it was evening everyone came to help Mrs Flummage catch her. As far as I know they still come every evening, without fail.

Alfred's New Diet

Alfred was a big, shaggy ant-eater with a long nose. His sticky tongue was as long as a ruler.

Alfred was always hungry. His best friend, Toucan, took him aside one day and said firmly, 'Alfred, I'm worried about you. I don't see how you can survive on ants. It's no wonder you are always hungry – you have to work so hard to catch them. I thought you might like to try a new diet.'

'But I *like* ants,' replied Alfred. 'Thank you for troubling yourself, Toucan, but I really can't think of anything I would rather eat.'

'Well,' said Toucan, 'not far from here, there is a hollow tree which is full of fat, juicy beetles. Much better for you old fellow! Come on.'

When they reached the tree, Alfred said gruffly, 'It doesn't look hollow to me. How do we get inside?'

'Come around here,' called Toucan from the other side of the tree. 'There's a hole just big enough to fit your nose through.'

Carefully, Alfred pushed his nose inside the tree.

'Ugh, these beetles taste horrid,' he shouted over his shoulder to Toucan. 'I'm coming out.'

But, when he tried to back away from the tree, his nose would not move.

'Toucan,' he yelled, 'help! My nose is stuck fast.'

Toucan grabbed Alfred's back leg with his beak and pulled as hard as he could. Alfred's nose still would not move.

'Hold on Alfred,' said Toucan, 'I'll be back in a minute.'

'Oh dear,' moaned Alfred. 'My nose is hurting.'

A few minutes later Toucan appeared, followed by Alfred's best friends. Toucan hopped up on to Alfred's back and directed the others.

'Anaconda, you wrap yourself once around Alfred's back legs. Llama, I'd like you to hang on to Anaconda. Crocodile, you hold on to Llama, and Jaguar, you go on the end. Now pull, everybody!'

They all pulled as hard as they could. Suddenly, Alfred's nose came unstuck and all his friends fell in a jumbled heap behind him.

'Hurrah!' cried Toucan, as all the animals picked themselves up and congratulated each other.

Alfred sat massaging his nose. 'Thank you everyone,' he said. 'And now I feel hungry enough for a nice big breakfast of ants. Would anyone care to join me?'

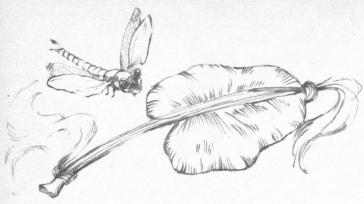

The Frankie Frog Five

Frankie Frog and his friends were in trouble. Their noisy games had upset everyone who lived in the Lily Pond. At last, Frankie's father told them that if they could not behave, they would be kept indoors.

'What can we do now?' said Albert. Frankie thought hard.

'I know!' he said suddenly. 'We'll give a concert! We'll invite everyone who lives in the Lily Pond to come and hear us making music!'

'A concert!' Albert was not sure, nor were Cyril, Wilfred and Harold.

'Why not?' demanded Frankie. 'I, for one, have a remarkably fine singing voice! Just listen!' And he tried out a few songs. 'But there's something not quite right about this last song . . .' he frowned. 'I *know!*' And he jumped so high into the air that he almost flew out of sight.

'You know *what?*' demanded Albert crossly, when Frankie landed again.

'*Guitars!*' shouted Frankie. 'That's what we need, to make a really good show! *Guitars!* Harold! Go and bring some young water-lily leaves! And Albert, get some thread from that old spider's web.'

Frankie and his friends set to work. They coated the spider thread with tree bark sap, to make it strong. Then they strung it carefully over a stiff young water-lily leaf. When it was quite dry, Frankie picked it up, and gently pulled the strings. It made a beautiful, loud *twang* and Frankie was delighted.

'Oh dear!' groaned Frankie's father.

'What will those boys do next?'

The morning of the concert was fine and dry, and, out of curiosity, the ducklings and the moorhens and the other frog families who lived in the Lily Pond came along to listen. Frankie's father came too, his ears well stuffed with lily-petals.

The Group played gaily:

'*Down by the Lily Pond, early in the morning,*
Watch those frogs all twist and jive!
Dig that beat and hum that music!
Listen folks! It's the Frankie Frog Five!'

The ducklings leapt up and cheeped noisily. The young moorhens shrieked, and even old Water Rat began a creaky little jig. All the birds for miles around flew into the overhanging tree branches and flapped their wings.

'What in the world has got into them all?' thought Frankie's father who couldn't hear anything.

Then he saw a very fat toad pushing his way towards him through the crowd. He was smoking a large cigar.

'I want a word with you!' he shouted at Frankie's father. 'Right now!'

'I've never heard anything like it!' he gasped, tapping ash from his cigar.

'I am sure you haven't!' agreed Frankie's father, unhappily.

'Marvellous!' the stranger was muttering. 'Simply marvellous! Allow me to introduce myself. I am Thomas T. Toad, of Toadstool Television! I want to offer those boys a contract!'

'A contract!' repeated Frankie's father weakly. 'You want to give them a *contract?*'

'That's what I said,' said Thomas T. Toad cheerfully. 'Why, those boys will be seen on every Toadstool Television screen in the country. Fabulous name too! The Frankie Frog Five! What about it?'

But for once, Frankie's father could not say a single word!

Long, Juicy Grass

Farmer Billings had a farm right in the middle of a sleepy valley. On one side of the valley, the slopes were covered with tall, green pine trees, as far as the eye could see. On the other side, the slopes were bare. Just one twisty, winding road climbed up the side, all the way from the bottom, right up over the hill.

Once a week, Farmer Billings climbed into his squeaky, creaky truck and drove to market up the twisty, winding road and over the top of the hill.

One morning, as Farmer Billings drove off to market, Gulliver, his cart-horse and Sarabell, his gentle brown cow, watched him from under their favourite tree.

'I have often wondered,' said Gulliver to Sarabell, 'what lies over that hill. Do you know?'

'Mmm,' mooed Sarabell dreamily, gazing thoughtfully towards the sky. 'I feel quite sure you will find long, juicy grass and golden buttercups there.'

'That does sound nice,' said Gulliver. 'Let us climb the hill and see for ourselves. Farmer Billings won't be back until the end of the day.'

So the two friends set off across the field towards the hill. On the way they met Buff the goat.

'Where are you off to?' asked Buff.

'We are going over the hill,' replied Gulliver, 'to find long, juicy grass and golden buttercups.'

'That does sound nice,' said Buff. 'Are there any crunchy thistles, too?'

'Sure to be,' mooed Sarabell.

'Then I'll come along,' said Buff.

So the three friends walked together to the foot of the hill. There they met Dixon the Duck splashing about in a puddle of water.

'Where are you off to?' quacked Dixon.

'We are going over the hill,' replied Gulliver, 'to find long, juicy grass, golden buttercups and crunchy thistles.'

'That does sound nice,' said Dixon. 'Are there any plump, pink worms, too?'

'Masses of them,' mooed Sarabell.

'Then I'll come along,' said Dixon.

So the four friends began to climb the hill. The sun shone down on them as they struggled up the twisty, winding road. It took them a long time and just before they reached the top, they were so tired that they all flopped down on the grass and fell asleep.

Gulliver was the first to wake and he trotted up to the top of the hill and looked over.

Sarabell woke up then and called, 'Have you found the long, juicy grass and golden buttercups?'

'No,' said Gulliver.

'Crunchy thistles?' shouted Buff, getting up from the grass.

'No,' said Gulliver.

'How about plump, pink worms?' puffed Dixon, waddling up to the brow of the hill.

'No,' said Gulliver, 'but come and see for yourselves!'

And they did.

There, below them, the hill sloped down gently to a soft, sandy beach and beyond that, to a blue, sparkling sea.

'So *that's* what lies over the hill!' they shouted. And the four friends ran and tumbled and galloped down the hummocky hill to the edge of the sea, where they splashed and played in the foamy waves until it was time to go.

On the way back, they met Farmer Billings coming along the road in his squeaky, creaky truck. What a surprise he got to see them! When Gulliver explained that they had gone to find out what was on the other side of the hill, Farmer Billings laughed.

'Well,' he said, 'I could have told you *that*! Now, hop in the back of my truck and we'll all go home.'

Birds in the Garden

Timothy lived in a big town. In the middle of the town was a square where lots of pigeons gathered. Every day his mummy would take him to the square to see the pigeons, and Timothy made friends with them. There was a lady in the square who sold special bird-food in bags and, if Timothy had saved enough pocket-money, he would buy some and toss it to the pigeons. They always seemed to be hungry.

Near the square in the town, there was a park, with a big duck pond. Timothy's mummy would save any left-over bread, and she and Timothy would feed it to the ducks. It was fun to see all the ducks racing across the water to gobble it up.

Also in the park, there was an aviary full of budgerigars. There were blue ones and greeny-yellow ones. Timothy and Mummy loved to watch the brightly coloured little birds as they darted about the big cage, twittering happily.

Now, Timothy's daddy was a teacher in the town. One day, he said, 'Timothy, I am going to leave the town school and teach at another school – a school in the countryside. We are going to move from the town and live in the country.'

Timothy couldn't help feeling rather sad at first.

'How I shall miss all my bird friends in the town!' he sighed to himself. 'I shan't see the hungry pigeons any more, or the ducks, or the pretty budgerigars.'

Mummy told him not to worry, for she was sure he would like living in the country.

At last, the day came for Timothy's family to move from their town home. Timothy went to the square to say good-bye to the pigeons, and then he went to the park to see the ducks and the budgerigars. When Timothy's family arrived at the house in the country, he found that it was very like their old house in the town, except that it had a lovely big garden with an apple tree.

While Timothy was in the kitchen having breakfast on their very first morning in the new house, he looked out of the window, and saw a robin fly down on to the lawn. The robin had come to peck at the toast-crusts Mummy had put there. After the robin, came a big blackbird, and then another bird that Mummy said was a thrush. The blackbird often came to sit in the apple tree, and he sang beautifully. The robin came every day, and soon he was so friendly that he settled on the window-sills, and looked curiously into the house.

The thrush came often, too, and he brought his family with him. In fact, the garden always seemed to be full of birds, and Timothy enjoyed watching them so much that he had no time to miss the town birds.

One day, Timothy said to Mummy and Daddy, 'I think that my friends the pigeons, the ducks and the budgerigars must have sent special bird-messages to the birds in the country, telling them to come and visit me, because they knew that I liked birds so much.'

Mummy smiled and said she was sure he was right!

A Special Touch of Magic

John was a big boy now. He was six years old. On his birthday his grandfather, who was a bit of a wizard, said, 'I'll take you to the fair. Here's a new ten pence piece to spend. Take good care of it – it's special.'

'Now, none of your tricks, Grandfather,' warned John's mother as she waved them off. 'And don't be late for tea!'

John and his grandfather walked across the fields. They could hear the music from the fair and John could just see the top of the big wheel over the hedges.

As they drew nearer, a strange yellow mist came down. Then, to John's great surprise, out of the mist appeared a wonderful roundabout.

On it there were dragons and monsters and turtles and dolphins and, the most beautiful of all – a roundabout horse with white flashing eyes.

In the middle of the roundabout sat a strange little man. Apart from him, the roundabout was empty.

John was just a little bit afraid and he reached out for his grandfather's hand – but Grandfather had disappeared!

'Come aboard, come aboard,' cooed the strange little man. 'Ten pence a time for the ride of your life.'

Somehow, John felt his legs climbing the roundabout steps. He gave the little man his bright new coin and sat on the horse with flashing eyes. No sooner had he done so, than the horse turned his head and winked at him!

'Hold tight,' he said. 'We're off!'

The little man had pushed a lever and the roundabout began to whirl.

'Oh my, this is fun!' shrieked John.

After a while, quite suddenly, the roundabout stopped and John found himself standing on the ground with Grandfather beside him.

'Time to go,' said Grandfather.

'Goodbye,' said John turning to wave to the roundabout horse. But the horse and the roundabout had disappeared.

'That's odd,' said John.

Walking home across the fields, John felt something in his pocket. It was the bright, new ten pence piece John had given to the roundabout man.

John looked at his grandfather in a puzzled way but Grandfather, who was a bit of a wizard, just smiled and said, 'I told you it was special.'

An Important Puppy

Paddy the puppy was sad. He had always been so happy playing with Michael and Susan and little Peter.

But yesterday the children's mother came home with a round, white, fluffy bundle and everybody forgot about Paddy. They just stared and laughed with delight at this new thing.

When no one was looking he decided he would find out what it was.

Paddy was puzzled. He could hear strange little noises coming from the cot where the bundle had been placed.

'Perhaps it is a kitten,' he thought, and he sniffed carefully around the cot. 'Or perhaps it is a mouse.'

And he barked to see what would happen. 'No, it can't be a mouse,' he decided. 'They wouldn't make all that fuss about a mouse.'

Then he thought, 'Suppose it is a new puppy that has come to take my place?'

He stood up and tried to peer into the cot but it was much too high for him. At last he went away and hid in his basket.

He was so unhappy he could not even eat his dinner! Suddenly, the children burst into the room.

'Ah, there you are, Paddy!' they cried. 'We have been looking everywhere for you – do come and see.'

Michael lifted him up so that he could look into the cot.

'Woof!' barked Paddy. 'It isn't a kitten, or a mouse, or another puppy. It's a little baby!'

'You will have to guard our new baby,' laughed Susan.

'Like a grown-up dog,' added Peter.

Paddy sat proudly by the side of the baby's cot. 'Now I am really important,' he thought to himself.

Violet and the Wicked Dog

Violet, the cow, was only about half as big as the other cows in the herd. They were all huge black-and-white Friesians, while Violet was a small, golden Jersey cow. Farmer Hoskins called her Violet because she was small and shy.

'Just like a violet,' he said.

Violet did not live with the other cows. Her home was in the meadow behind the farm-house. She gave rich milk, with lots of cream on the top. Mrs Hoskins said that Violet must be a 'house cow', to supply lots of creamy milk.

So Violet shared the meadow with chicken, ducks, geese, bantams, a few sheep and the farm dogs.

Down in the village lived a big, black, bristly dog called Growler. Growler was a bully – he fought the dogs on the farm; he chased the cats and the fowls and the ducks; he drove the sheep into hedges, where they became tangled up in brambles. When Violet saw him coming, she went and hid in her shed.

'I wish we could do something about that wicked dog,' sighed Farmer Hoskins.

One night, Violet had a calf. It was a lovely little fawny-gold calf, with a white star in the middle of its forehead. In the morning it curled up in the sunshine, under the pink and white blossom on the apple-trees, and went to sleep. So Violet wandered off to graze.

Suddenly, Growler came charging into the meadow. All the chickens, ducks, cats and sheep ran away to hide. The dogs crept under the barn. Growler looked around and caught sight of the little calf, asleep under the trees. Here was a new animal he could bully. He bounded across the grass, barking.

The little calf climbed to its feet and stood there, wobbling. 'Maaaaa!' it said.

Instantly, Violet turned to see what was frightening her precious calf.

No animal ever ran faster than Violet. She hurtled across the meadow like an express train. She lowered her head and . . . *whack* . . . she hit Growler before he even knew she was coming. Then she hit him again, and again, and again. Growler howled and yelped. He put his tail between his legs and ran for his life. Violet chased after him and with one last mighty butt sent him head over heels into the river. Then she went trotting back, to comfort her calf.

From that day on, Growler was terrified of Violet and he never came into the farmyard again.

Birthday Stripes

Charlie Monkey was always teasing, and at times all the other animals in the forest felt very cross with him.

He used to jump on to Elephant's back time after time to see how far he could go before Elephant realised that he was there.

Sometimes, if Giraffe was walking in the forest, Charlie would run high up along the branches of the trees until Giraffe's little horns and ears appeared through a gap in the leaves. Then Charlie would shoot out his arm and tickle Giraffe's horns or whisper in his ear or even slide down his long neck.

Hippo, too, used to get very angry with Charlie, who liked to throw nuts at him when he was bathing in the water.

All the same, the animals loved Charlie because he was kind and generous, and always full of fun.

One afternoon, Charlie knew that the next day must be Grumps the tiger's birthday. Charlie had crept up behind Grumps, meaning to take him by surprise. As Grumps was rather old and irritable, Charlie didn't want to frighten him too much, so he pattered slowly and softly through the cool leaves into the clearing where Grumps was sitting licking each stripe and counting to himself.

Charlie knew that the old tiger only did that once a year – the day before his birthday. So, instead of startling him, he crept back into the trees and started to think about birthdays. Then he called the other animals to him.

'Everybody, listen to me,' said Charlie. 'Shall we give Grumps a present for his birthday?'

'Grumps is too old to have any more birthdays,' said Laura the lazy leopard.

'You're always teasing us – how do we really know it's his birthday?' said Giraffe, swinging his long neck.

Nobody seemed very interested, so Charlie went away to think by himself. Night fell and he was sitting in a tree, still thinking of what to give Grumps for a present. Suddenly, he saw something far below him on the forest lake. There on the dark water were twinkles of light, sparkling and shining.

'Precious stones!' thought Charlie in excitement. 'Treasure!' It looked as if silver jewels had fallen from the sky and the little monkey was very excited. He thought these would be a wonderful present for Grumps.

He slithered down the tree until he reached a low branch that overhung the water. The treasure winked at him from the surface of the water.

Charlie leaned out from his branch. Further, further he stretched until he was almost upside down. He reached out his long arm to take one of the jewels, but he leaned a little too far and toppled into the water with a long, loud, SPLASH!

Poor Charlie bobbed up and down in the water, spluttering, shouting, sneezing and waving his arms and legs all ways at once.

The other animals all arrived to see what was happening. Kind Hippo, who liked a bath at any time of night, lumbered in to rescue Charlie who was shouting, 'My treasure! My jewels! They fell from the sky!'

'Jewels?' inquired Laura the leopard, interested.

'Treasure from the sky?' asked Giraffe. 'I'm nearer the sky than any of you and I've never seen any.'

'I can only see stars up there,' said Elephant, blowing through his trunk to dry Charlie's wet fur. 'Look, they're reflected in the water.'

'Stars.' Charlie looked sad. 'That's all they were. And I really thought they were precious stones that I could give to Grumps for his birthday.'

Everyone went quiet and looked to see if Grumps was there listening. He was. The old tiger was standing in the shadows laughing . . . shaking with laughter . . . ROARING with laughter.

'You've given me the best birthday present I've ever had,' he said. 'I haven't laughed like that for years. I feel ten stripes younger! Tomorrow on my birthday I shall think of how funny you looked, Charlie Monkey, and how kind you were to want to give me a present. And we can all share the treasure – since the stars are always there for us to see. Now, it's time you were in bed, Charlie Monkey. You have to help me celebrate my birthday tomorrow, remember!'

Charlie felt much happier, and because Grumps was old and wise, he did as he was told – just for once.

A Change
in the Weather

Dylan the weathercock lived on the church steeple. He was painted gold and spun with the wind day and night. Everyone in the village was fond of his familiar figure turning this way and that, to show which direction the wind was coming from.

The north and east winds brought cold weather so that when Dylan's beak pointed towards 'N' or 'E' the village folk turned up their collars and pulled their scarves more tightly round their necks.

If Dylan spun to the west, people took their umbrellas out with them because the west wind brought rain. He liked spinning to the south best of all because the soft south breeze brought sunshine and fine, warm weather.

One day Dylan looked down at the farmyard below him near the church and saw all the animals playing and feeding and chattering together.

'That does look fun,' he thought. 'I get so lonely here. I wonder if anyone would take my place for a little while so that I could go and be a farm cockerel for a few days.'

He could not imagine any of the farm animals on top of the church steeple. 'Ducks sit on water,' he thought, 'and hens sit on their chicks, not on church steeples. And I've heard of a cow who

jumped over the moon, but not one who can climb a church steeple!'

So one evening he asked the owl if he would like to come and tell the weather for a few days. The owl said he could come at night but he preferred to go to sleep during the day.

'That's no good,' said Dylan. 'Everyone else is asleep at night.'

He invited a passing pigeon to take his place. 'Yes, I'll come,' said the pigeon. 'I shall have a lovely view of the farmer's cabbages and when he's not looking, I can fly down and eat them.'

'No! No! That won't do at all,' said Dylan, and sent the pigeon right away.

A seagull flew into the village on the cold wind from the sea and said he would love to come and look after the weather for a little while. Sitting on top of a church would be a nice change from sitting on a cliff.

So Dylan flew down to the farmyard and joined the animals there. He crowed loudly at them from the roof of a barn:

'Cock-a-doodle-doo!
I've come to visit you.
N-E-W-S of the weather I bring;
For North, East, West or South
There is a song that I will sing.'

Dylan strutted about in the farmyard feeling rather important. The animals all thought he was very clever.

'Tell us the weather,' they pleaded, crowding round him, and he felt proud. But then he felt puzzled – he couldn't feel where the wind was coming from because the farmyard was too sheltered. But he would have felt very embarrassed to admit that he did not know, so he pretended and sang:

'N-E-W-S of the weather today!
South wind, warm,
You'll come to no harm.'

The cows were pleased to hear this and lay about in the field. Mother Hen took her chicks for a walk. The ducks got ready to go swimming and the sheep sent their lambs out to play. And then, to everyone's surprise, the sky turned dark, the wind blew cold and it began to snow. The animals were furious with Dylan.

'You're no good! Go home, cocky Dylan!' they cried, mooing and bleating and quacking at him.

Dylan felt ashamed and wanted to go home. He told the animals he was sorry for showing off and disturbing them.

He flew back to the church steeple where the seagull greeted him cheerfully.

'I'm glad you're back,' he said. 'I'm tired of being a weather-gull. I've been hot and cold and very dizzy all the time from spinning around. I'm going home to the seaside to my cliff-top.'

The seagull flew away through the snowflakes and Dylan settled happily on top of the church again. Although the wind was cold, he felt warm and happy inside as the wind swung him gently on the weather vane. He crowed softly:

'East, West,
Home's best.
Rain or shine,
This place is mine!'

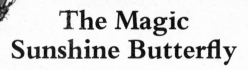

The Magic Sunshine Butterfly

Mary sat very still watching the butterfly in the garden. It stood poised on a flower, its delicate, colourful wings fanning the air as the sunbeams danced around it. It was so beautiful that Mary knew it must be a magic butterfly. She called it Priscilla.

Mary would hold out her hand to Priscilla, and the butterfly would flutter over and rest on her finger, fanning her wings gently. But she would only stay a moment, and then she would fly off and settle on a rose.

One day, Mary went to visit her grandfather, who lived high on a hill not far from Mary's house. When she reached the house, she rang the bell and was surprised when her grandfather did not answer the door. His housekeeper, Mrs Finch, answered it instead.

Mrs Finch told her that her grandfather had been ill and was still not feeling well. Mary went in to see him, and sat by his bed.

'Oh, I should love to see the sunshine,' her grandfather sighed. 'I have not seen a green leaf, a flower, grass, or any of the little creatures of the wood, for such a long time. This room is so dark. I am sure I would get better quickly if I could see a little sunshine.'

Suddenly, Mary thought of a way to make her grandfather happy.

She walked back to her garden, where she saw Priscilla poised on a red rose. She was looking more beautiful than ever, with her brightly coloured wings shimmering in the sun. Priscilla flew to Mary's shoulder and stayed there. Mary walked back happily to her grandfather's house.

When Mrs Finch opened the door, she stared in amazement at the beautiful butterfly resting on Mary's shoulder. As soon as Mary walked into her grandfather's room with Priscilla, the room seemed to be filled with dancing golden sunbeams.

'I've come to show you my Magic Sunshine Butterfly, Grandfather,' said Mary, brightly.

'She's beautiful,' said her grandfather, sitting up to enjoy the sunshine, 'and I feel better already.'

Bluebird and Pinkwings

There was a sad little bird in the forest. His name was Bluebird, and he had lost his singing voice. He was so unhappy that he went to tell Fairy Pinkwings what had happened.

'Bad Fairy Brownwing cast one of her spells on me to stop me singing,' sighed Bluebird. 'I don't suppose I shall ever be able to sing again.'

'Yes, you will,' promised Pinkwings. 'Wait there while I fetch my book of good spells from Fairyland.'

At last, Pinkwings came back with her big book of good spells. She turned to the page on Lost Voices and, standing facing Bluebird, she said a magic spell:

'Fairyland magic of my choice,
Bring this Bluebird back his voice!'

Pinkwings waved her magic wand and at once Bluebird began to sing happily. The fairy flew away before he had a chance to thank her, but he made up his mind to repay her for her help. His chance came when, a few weeks later, he saw Fairy Pinkwings sitting unhappily in the forest.

'I caught one of my wings on a prickly bush,' she said. 'It is torn a little and I can't fly. The only place where I can get a new wing is the Fairy Queen's Palace, but that's far away in Fairyland.'

Bluebird told Pinkwings to climb on his back, and he flew her all the way to Fairyland. The Fairy Queen soon found a lovely new wing for Pinkwings. It matched her other wing perfectly.

'Please stay for the Fairy Ball tonight, Bluebird,' said the Fairy Queen.

Bluebird did stay, and when it was Pinkwings' turn to dance her fairy dance, he sang for her. The Fairy Queen and all the fairies and pixies at the ball agreed that Pinkwings was the prettiest fairy of all, and they agreed that Bluebird had the loveliest singing voice they had ever listened to!

Samantha and the King of the Mice

Many years ago a little girl called Samantha lived with her parents in a tiny house. They were very poor, but Samantha was a happy little girl and she always enjoyed herself.

One day as she was playing in the garden, she heard a strange noise by the gate.

'Ho, ho, hum,' said the gatepost. 'That was a nice snooze. But now that I am awake, I am very hungry.'

'Gateposts can't talk,' said Samantha. She was very surprised. 'They should not be hungry, either.'

'What a funny child, talking to a gatepost!' said the same voice. A little old elf jumped from behind the gatepost.

'That was *me* talking,' he said. 'I am hungry. Do you have some cheese?'

Samantha ran into the house and took a piece of cheese from the table. Then she ran back to the little elf.

The elf was very pleased. 'Now I owe you a wish,' he said. 'I am the King of the Mice.' Then he disappeared behind the gatepost. Samantha looked carefully, but she could not find him anywhere.

Her mother was very cross when Samantha told her about the cheese. 'You are very naughty to give away the cheese without asking me first,' she said.

Poor Samantha was sent to bed without any food. 'Oh dear,' she sobbed unhappily, 'I do wish we were not so poor.'

'That's a very easy wish,' said a little voice and in through the window came the elf. 'You shall have your wish,' he said. Then he disappeared again.

A moment later, Samantha heard a great shriek from the kitchen. She ran downstairs and what a sight she saw! There was her mother standing on the table. The kitchen was full of mice!

The King of the Mice was there too. 'Do please be quiet,' he said to Samantha's mother. 'We are bringing you some treasure. You should be pleased.'

Then in through the door came a hundred more mice. They were carrying a little gold purse. The King of the Mice gave the purse to Samantha. Inside was a big gold coin.

'That is a magic purse,' he said. 'If you are good and kind, you will find a new coin in the purse every day. If you are mean or naughty, you will never find any more coins in it.' Then he ran out of the door and all the mice followed him, chattering and squeaking noisily.

Samantha's mother was so surprised that she had forgotten to be frightened of the mice. And when Samantha's father came home, she told him all about the magic purse and Samantha's friend, the King of the Mice.

'Hooray,' cried Samantha's father. 'We are rich! Let's go out this afternoon to spend the magic coin.'

They went to town to spend their gold coin. They bought lots of food and the biggest, roundest cheese in the whole of the town.

They took the cheese home and put it in the middle of their garden. Suddenly, out popped the King of the Mice from behind some flowers, followed by hundreds of little mice. They had a tremendous feast of cheese and the King of the Mice had the most. He had an enormous appetite for an elf!

Every day after that, Samantha and her parents found another gold coin in the magic purse. Every day, too, they bought another big cheese for the mice.

Rusty's New Trick

'I wish Rusty would carry a parcel like that,' said David, pointing to a spaniel trotting along the pavement with a parcel in its mouth.

'We could train him,' said Betty, giving their pet terrier a pat. 'He is intelligent.'

A few days later Betty and David gave Rusty a good report.

'Nine out of ten. He only dropped the parcel once,' said David.

'But he only carried it the length of the hall,' Dad replied. 'I wouldn't trust that dog with a parcel of mine.'

'Well, we're going to take a birthday present to Granny tomorrow, and Rusty is going to carry it,' said Betty.

The following day Mummy took out the pink bed-socks she had knitted for Granny, and Betty wrote on a card: 'To Granny, 27 Gables Avenue. Happy Birthday.' Then she wrapped them in brown paper and said, 'Here, Rusty! Take it to Granny.'

Rusty sniffed at the parcel, then he took it in his mouth.

'Come on, boy!' cried David, running down the garden path.

Rusty followed obediently until he saw Trixie, the next-door cat. He dropped the parcel and rushed after her, yapping loudly.

Betty and David ran after him. A few minutes later the parcel was back between Rusty's jaws.

They were near a cottage at the end of the road when a car pulled up beside them.

'Hello, there!' called a cheery voice. 'That's a clever dog you've got there!'

'Uncle Brian!' cried the children, and they told him all about Rusty's new trick and Granny's present.

When Uncle Brian had gone, David looked round for Rusty.

'He was here a minute ago,' said Betty.

Rusty suddenly emerged from the old cottage garden.

'There he is,' said Betty. 'And he still has the parcel.'

'Well, I think I'll carry it now until we reach Granny's gate,' decided David.

Once they were inside Granny's garden they gave Rusty the parcel again.

'Happy birthday!' called Betty when Granny came to the door. 'Rusty is going to give you your present.'

'I wonder what it can be,' said Granny.

Then she slowly opened the parcel. There was a gasp of surprise. The brown paper contained a chop bone, some fish skin and cheese rind.

'It's the wrong parcel!' said David.

'Oh! Ha-ha-ha!' roared Grandpa.

Granny's shoulders began to shake, and soon she was wiping tears of laughter from her eyes. Then there came a knock on the door. It was Miss Timmings, from the cottage down the road. She was a friend of Granny's.

'I found this parcel on my garden path,' she said. 'It has your name inside, so I brought it along. Nice bed-socks!'

'Nicer than these,' chuckled Granny, pointing to the contents of her parcel.

'Oh! Those look like the scraps a friend leaves on the doorstep for my cats,' said Miss Timmings.

Betty and David looked at each other. 'Rusty ran into someone's garden while we talked to Uncle Brian,' David said.

'And found something more to his taste than bed-socks,' declared Grandpa.

'Never mind!' smiled Granny as she exchanged parcels with Miss Timmings. 'The bed-socks are just what I wanted, and Rusty's new trick has given me the best laugh of my birthday.'

The Kitten

Andrew and Jane were brother and sister, and they had a beautiful cat. One day in the spring, the cat disappeared. The children looked for her everywhere, but they could not find her.

When they were playing near the barn weeks later, they heard the sound of tiny miaows coming from somewhere up above. Andrew climbed the ladder to the roof of the barn, while Jane stood below, asking, 'Have you found her?'

At last Andrew called down to her excitedly, 'I've found her. It's our cat . . . and she has kittens. Come up and have a look!' And he helped her up the ladder.

There were three kittens altogether. The children chose one of them as their favourite – a grey one with white paws – and asked their mother if they could keep it. She said they could as long as they looked after it very carefully.

One day, the children went out to play and they took their kitten with them. The wind was stirring the leaves in the lane, and the children enjoyed watching the kitten play with them. Then they found some flowers growing beside the road and began to pick them, forgetting all about their kitten. Suddenly, they heard someone shout, 'Come back, come back!' and they saw a hunter on horseback. His two dogs were running ahead of him and had seen the kitten.

Jane screamed when she saw the dogs and ran away, but Andrew ran to the kitten as fast as he could and snatched it up before the dogs could reach it.

The hunter said how sorry he was for frightening the kitten and then galloped away on his horse. Andrew and Jane carried the kitten home. They told their mother about their adventure and promised they would never play with the kitten outside in the lane again.

Daisy-May Goes Climbing

On summer afternoons people used to come in cars to see the church at Marytown. They sat in the churchyard and looked at the carvings and at the sundial over the church porch. But what they came to see more than anything else was the big willow bush growing from the top of the church tower.

'I wonder how it got there?' the children would say.

'I expect that a bird dropped the seed,' their parents would explain.

Don lived on a farm near the church in Marytown. He was a lucky little boy, for he had lots of animals as pets. He had a dog, several cats, some bantams, a goose, a hutch of guinea-pigs, and a goat. The goat's name was Daisy-May.

Daisy-May was greedy, like all goats. When she saw anything new, the first thing she did was to try to eat it. So, when the latch on the gate broke and Dad tied a rope around the gate until the latch could be mended, Daisy-May ate the rope. The gate swung open and she trotted out.

Nobody missed her until Don came home from school. Then he happened to look up at the church tower, and there on the very top was Daisy-May! She was eating the willow bush.

Don rushed indoors.

'Come and look! Come and look at Daisy-May,' he cried.

Everyone came out to see.

'Somebody must have left the church door open,' said Mummy.

'Did she climb up all those little stone steps inside the tower?' asked Don.

'She must have done,' said his mother.

'And now she will have to walk back down again,' said his father.

But Daisy-May refused. She liked going up, but she did not like coming down. She made such a fuss that, in the end, Dad and three other men had to tie a big sack around her and lower her from the tower on the end of a rope.

Daisy-May struggled and bleated all the way down, but nobody felt sorry for her. No visitors come to see the bush growing on top of the tower now, because Daisy-May ate it that day.

Rainy Day Rhythm

Clip clop, splish splosh. Duncan the big grey cart horse was trotting along in the rain. Splatter patter, splatter patter. Duffy the sheepdog was trotting along in the rain. 'Tra-la-tra-lee,' sang Tom, the farmer's boy, riding along the lane, on Duncan's back.

Duncan had been pulling cart-loads of corn all day from the field to the tall, red barn in the farmyard. Tom had helped his father and the farm hands unload the corn from the cart and pile it high in the barn. Duffy had been busy, too, chasing rabbits.

Just as the last cart-load of corn had been stored inside the barn, it had started to rain.

Duncan had felt the first drops dribble down his ears and right down his long, grey nose. Duffy had stopped chasing rabbits and had tried to catch raindrops instead. Tom had cupped both hands together and had tried to catch some, too, but it trickled through his fingers.

Tom's father said, 'Quick, Tom! I'll unhitch Duncan from the cart, then you can take him home.'

And that was how Duncan came to be clip clopping, splish sploshing along the road in the rain, with Duffy splatter pattering by his side and Tom, singing tra-la-tra-lee, at the top of his voice, all the way home.

When they got home, Tom took Duncan to his stable and gave him a bag of hay and a bowl of oats. Then he filled a bucket of water for Duncan to drink and, last of all, Tom spread lots of new, sweet-smelling straw in the stable for him to lie on.

By the time he had finished doing all that, the rain had stopped.

'No more splatter pattering for you,' said Tom to Duffy, as he closed the stable door.

'And no more tra-la-tra-leeing for *you*,' laughed Tom's father, who had come to see that all was well for the night. 'Now, come along both of you for a well-earned supper!'

The Birthday Puppy

As soon as Mark opened his eyes, he remembered that it was a special day – his birthday!

He sat up in his bed. His eyes widened when he saw something on the floor near the door. It was a round, flat basket and inside the basket was a white puppy with black patches on it. The puppy was fast asleep.

Mark crept across and leaned over the basket. The puppy opened one eye, twitched its ears, and gave a little wag of its tail. Then it went to sleep again.

Mark rushed in to see his parents.

'Mummy . . . Daddy . . .' he shouted. 'There's a puppy in my room. Is he mine?'

'Yes, Mark,' answered Mummy. 'And you must look after him yourself, but Daddy and I will help you.'

'What are you going to call the puppy?' asked Mummy.

Mark thought hard, then said, 'Patch, because he has black patches.'

When he had dressed and had eaten his breakfast, Mark took Patch out into the garden to play. Patch raced round and round the lawn; then he started to dig in the vegetable patch. Mark thought Daddy would not be very pleased if he saw that, so he made him stop digging. Instead, Patch tried to jump over the flowers, but he landed 'flop' in the middle. Mark was beginning to feel worried, so he said, 'I know. I'll take you for a walk, Patch.'

Patch looked up at him eagerly, wagging his tail. Mark knew that he never went out without Mummy. But Mummy had said he was to take Patch for walks – and it *was* his birthday. So he fetched the lead Mummy had bought for Patch and fastened it to his collar.

At first Patch did not want to walk. Mark had to pull very hard on the lead to make him move at all. Then, suddenly, he started to run. He ran very fast and Mark had to race along to keep up.

Soon they came to the supermarket, where Mark went shopping with Mummy. Patch rushed through the open door, towing a breathless Mark. *Crash* went a pile of tins! Mark tripped over and let go of the lead. Tins were rolling everywhere. Patch was frightened by the noise. He scampered away – straight into a stack of boxes full of washing powder, which fell noisily to the floor.

Mark was very frightened. What would everyone say when they knew that Patch belonged to him? And what would Mummy do?

'Are you the cause of all the trouble?' said a deep voice. It was the man Mummy called the Manager.

'Yes,' said Mark in a small voice. 'We're very sorry.'

Patch wriggled close to Mark and wagged a hopeful tail.

Then, the kind Manager smiled. 'Just this once, I'll forgive you. But you must never come out without Mummy again. Now I'll take you home.'

So Mark and Patch climbed into the Manager's car and were driven home. At first Mark thought Mummy was going to be cross, but after talking to the Manager she turned to Mark with a smile.

'I don't think you'll be going out alone again, but come along now and have a glass of milk,' said Mummy, kindly.

'And where has Patch gone?' asked the Manager.

They all looked and there he was, curled up fast asleep in the most comfortable chair. It had been a very exciting morning!

A Song for Princess Poppy

Mrs Blackbird looked down from the branch of a crab-apple tree where she had just decided to build herself a nest. What was all that laughter she could hear in the distance? As it grew nearer she could see quite clearly. Now, the pixies and elves were giving a big party that night in honour of Princess Poppy's birthday, and they were busy stringing coloured fairy-lights in the branches of the trees and bushes.

'You are not putting those things in my crab-apple tree,' chirruped the angry Mrs Blackbird. 'I am about to build a nest here and you will shake it out again.'

'Oh, but please, Mrs Blackbird,' called the pixies. 'Can't your nest wait until tomorrow? This part of the wood will be so dark if we do not light your tree.'

'No, no!' snapped the angry bird. 'It may rain tomorrow, and I hate working in the wet. I want to start now, while the sun is shining.' Looking sad, the pixies went away, and left Mrs Blackbird to start building her nest.

'What can we do to make her change her mind?' the pixies asked each other.

'I know,' said Trixie. 'Let's ask Mrs Thrush for her help. She may have an idea.'

Now Mrs Thrush had been invited to sing for Princess Poppy at the party that night and she was very excited about it. But when she heard the pixies' sad little tale, she very kindly said, 'I shall pretend to have a sore throat and I want you to ask the Princess to invite Mrs Blackbird to sing instead.'

'Oh, but we were so looking forward to hearing you sing,' cried the pixies.

'Never mind,' answered Mrs Thrush, 'I shall enjoy the party just the same.'

Later that morning, Trixie took the invitation to Mrs Blackbird. She was so surprised and delighted that she decided to put off building her nest until the next day after all. She decided to practise her songs instead.

'I am sorry I was so rude to you this morning,' she said. 'I would love you to decorate my crab-apple tree.'

That night, when the party was in full swing and the pixies were dancing beneath the twinkling lights, Mrs Blackbird's first song was announced. She was about to begin, when she spied Mrs Thrush sitting nearby. 'Would you join me in my songs?' asked Mrs Blackbird.

Mrs Thrush was just going to say she had a slight sore throat, when she remembered it was not really true. 'I would enjoy that very much,' she replied. 'My throat is better now.'

Then, to the great pleasure of the Princess and all her pixie guests, the two birds sang a beautiful song. Princess Poppy was so delighted that she placed a garland of daisies around the neck of each little bird, and thanked them both. She had no idea that Mrs Blackbird had nearly spoilt the party and the pixies never told her their secret.

The Cat
Who Went Fishing

'I'm going fishing with Jimmy and Bob,' said Billy at breakfast.

'Miaow!' said Timkin.

'I think he is asking to go with you!' said Mummy.

'I *can't* take him! What would the others say if I took a cat?' laughed Jimmy.

'No, I suppose you couldn't,' said Mummy. 'You will have to stay with me, Timkin.'

Timkin put his tail in the air, and walked out of the back door, looking very cross.

'What's wrong with Timkin?' asked Billy.

'He will be all right. I'll look after him,' said Mummy.

Just then, Jimmy and Bob came to the door, so Billy ran off to get his rod and line, and forgot about Timkin.

When Billy came home for dinner, Mummy said, 'Timkin has been away all morning, and hasn't come back yet!'

'Oh dear! I wish I'd taken him with me! We didn't catch anything but tiddlers all day, and we put those back,' explained Billy.

'Have your dinner, and then go and look for him,' said Mummy.

After dinner, Billy went and asked the local policeman if he had seen Timkin. He said, 'Timkin? Yes, I saw him very early this morning. He went down the road to the quay where the fishing boats dock.'

So Billy went down to the quay, and asked about Timkin there. The fishing boats were all out by this time, but an old man sitting on a coil of rope said, 'Timkin? Would that be a smart little black cat with a red collar?'

'Yes!' said Billy eagerly. 'Do you know where he is?'

The old man shook his head. 'He was walking down the quay, and he stopped and looked at every fishing boat. Maybe he's signed on as a mate on one!' The old man wheezed with laughter.

'Oh dear!' said Billy. 'Maybe he fell off the quay and drowned!'

The old man stopped laughing. 'Don't

you worry, sonny. Look, the boats are coming back. Maybe they'll have news for you.'

As the first boat came nearer, Billy rubbed his eyes. He could hardly believe what he saw. On the deck was Timkin with a fish in his mouth. The boat docked, and then a big man jumped down on to the quay, holding Timkin firmly in his arms.

'Timkin! What *have* you been up to?' gasped Billy.

'Oh, does he belong to you?' said the fisherman. 'Hope you haven't been worrying about him. He stowed himself away behind the fish boxes, and only came out when we were at sea! But he is good company, and can come with us whenever he likes!'

'Wait a minute,' went on the man, 'we've given him his share of the catch, but he couldn't carry much. Suppose you take this one, too.' He handed a big fish to Billy.

'Thank you very much!' said Billy. 'Come on now Timkin, let's go home.'

The Ducks Go Visiting

Drake and Duck lived on a farm in the country. They were very happy ducks – they had a comfortable house to sleep in, a big pond to swim on and plenty to eat. They also had lots of friends in the farm-yard and spent most of their day out visiting them all.

Drake and Duck were very punctual visitors. They always had breakfast with Porker the pig at exactly eight o'clock in the morning, a chat with Bill the goat at nine o'clock, morning tea with Nelly the horse at ten and a gossip with Martha the cow at eleven.

Porker, Bill, Nelly and Martha looked forward to seeing the ducks because they brought them little titbits of news about the farm.

One morning, Drake woke up, yawned and stretched, and looked outside their house.

'It's a beautiful day, Duck,' he said in a voice loud enough to wake her up. 'Perfect weather for visiting. Let's go and see Porker.'

They waddled over to Porker's sty. It seemed very quiet.

'Porker, are you there?' called Drake cheerfully. 'We've come for breakfast. Porker!'

But the only reply they heard was the sound of contented snoring. Drake and Duck peered through the slats in the gate and there, fast asleep inside, lay Porker.

'That's strange,' said Duck, 'it's not like Porker to eat breakfast without us. Come on Drake, we'll never be able to wake him.'

There was no sign of Bill the goat when Duck and Drake arrived at his field.

'Oh bother,' said Drake, stamping his foot, 'he must have gone into the other paddock. And I had something important to tell him, too.'

They waddled on to see Nelly and arrived just in time to see Farmer Tom hitching her to his cart.

Nelly looked annoyed. 'Hello,' she said, 'I'm afraid I can't stop now – I'm taking Farmer Tom to market.'

'Well,' said Duck, turning away disappointed, 'at least Martha will be there. We can tell her all the news.'

Martha had her back to them when they came up.

'Hello Martha,' said Drake.

Martha didn't even bother to look up as she said, 'It's my lunchtime now and I can't possibly talk while I'm eating.'

Duck and Drake waddled off down the hill to their pond feeling very hurt.

'I just can't understand it,' said Drake, shaking his head. Nobody wanted to see us today!'

To his amazement, Duck suddenly started to laugh. 'Oh Drake, we *are* silly. Look at the sun – it's nearly one o'clock in the afternoon. We must have woken up very late. No wonder all our friends were busy with other things. Tomorrow we'll make sure that we get up at the right time and then everyone will be happy!'

Tiny's New Dress

Tiny Squirrel had bought a lovely new dress, all ready for the warm summer weather. She kept peeping at it as it hung in the cupboard of her room in the chestnut tree. It was pink – Tiny's favourite colour.

One morning, her mother, Mrs Squirrel, put on her blue bonnet and red shawl and told Tiny she was going to visit an old friend.

'While I am gone I want you to go to Mushroom Market and call at the shop for some lettuce leaves,' she said.

When her mother had gone, Tiny remembered the new dress. It was a sunny day and she thought it would be fun to wear the dress for the first time. Tiny took her pink dress out of the cupboard and put it on, admiring herself in the mirror. Then she started out happily on the path to the shop.

Tiny really did look very pretty. But, suddenly, a dreadful thing happened. It began to rain! Tiny ran for shelter, but the nearest was only a very small, newly growing oak tree. It rained so hard that Tiny's pretty new dress was soon crumpled and spoilt.

Tiny Squirrel waited for the rain to stop and then, feeling very miserable, she crept home. And, when Mrs Squirrel arrived home, Tiny was in bed! Mrs Squirrel was very surprised but poor Tiny was so unhappy that she quite forgot to be cross. She set to work and ironed Tiny's dress and when she had finished, it looked as good as new again.

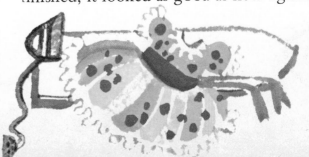

Hoppy Hare's Happy Birthday

Hoppy Hare's birthday was on April Fools' Day – the first day of April. But he never enjoyed it because the other animals always teased him and called him Foolish Hoppy. Then, one birthday morning, Hoppy had a wonderful idea.

'Yippee!' he shouted, and bounded off down the winding road which led to Farmer Penny's farm.

'You're in an awful hurry, Foolish Hoppy Hare,' grunted Percy Pig from a mud patch at the roadside. 'Going to a birthday party?'

Hoppy grinned at Percy.

'I'm off to see a pig swim across Farmer Penny's big pond.'

'But pigs don't swim,' grunted Percy.

'No matter, that's where I'm going,' chuckled Hoppy.

'Then I'm coming with you, for this should be worth seeing,' answered the pig, eagerly.

A little farther down the road, Greedy Goat was busy eating his breakfast as Hoppy and Percy went past.

'What's the hurry, Foolish Hoppy Hare?' asked the goat.

'We are off to see a pig and a goat in a swimming race on Farmer Penny's big pond,' said Hoppy.

'But goats don't swim,' replied Greedy, brusquely.

'No matter, that's where we're going.'

'Then I'm coming with you,' said the goat, 'for I've never before seen a goat and a pig in a race.'

Soon they met Grey Donkey nibbling at some thistles in the hedgerow.

'Hee-haw! Foolish Hoppy Hare. Why do you hurry?' brayed the donkey.

'We are off to see a swimming race between a pig, a goat, and a donkey on Farmer Penny's big pond.'

'But donkeys don't swim,' said Grey Donkey.

'No matter, that's where we're going.'

'Then I'm coming with you,' said the donkey, 'for I'm sure even the slowest of donkeys can go faster than either a pig or a goat.'

Around the next corner they met Susy Sheep.

'Baaaa! Foolish Hoppy Hare,' she called out. 'Where are you off to so early?'

'We're off to see a swimming race on Farmer Penny's big pond, between a pig, a goat, a donkey, and a sheep,' Hoppy Hare replied.

'But sheep don't swim,' said Susy.

'No matter, that's where we're going,' answered Hoppy.

'Then I'll come with you,' said Susy Sheep, following behind, 'for if a sheep can swim as fast as it can run, it will be sure to win.'

At last they came to the hedge which grew all the way round Farmer Penny's big pond.

'Now push your way through the hedge, and you will see the pond,' said Hoppy Hare. 'But hurry, it's time for the race.' And Hoppy very politely stood aside to let the others go in first.

But as the four of them jumped through the hedge, oh, what a surprise they got.

SPLASH went Percy Pig into the water.

SPLASH went Greedy Goat.

SPLASH went Grey Donkey.

SPLASH went Susy Sheep.

And as they splashed about in the deep, muddy pond, Hoppy Hare sat on the narrow bank and laughed and laughed.

'Help! Help!' they all cried out.

After he thought they had been in the water long enough, Hoppy very kindly fished them out with his long fishing line which he had hidden under the hedge.

'Whoever heard of a pig, a goat, a donkey, and a sheep in a swimming race?' he teased, as they dried themselves out in the sun.

And do you know, that was the very last time they called him Foolish Hoppy Hare on his birthday.

Hunt the Carrots

One morning at the breakfast table, Mrs Rabbit was complaining to her family about the price of vegetables. 'Just look at that,' she said, waving a paw at *The Woodland Echo*. 'Carrots have gone up by four pence a pound since last week. If they get any dearer I shall have to buy one at a time!'

Mr Rabbit thought about this worrying problem for a moment, while Mrs Rabbit continued to read her paper. Then he had a bright idea. 'Why don't we grow our own carrots,' he suggested. 'We could grow as many as we could eat in our little garden and it wouldn't cost us very much money at all.'

Mrs Rabbit and the five bunny children thought this was a splendid idea and everyone offered to help.

That morning, they all set off for the shops. First they went to the bookshop and bought a book all about growing vegetables. Then they went to Bill Badger's garden shop and chose some packets of carrot seeds, which Bill Badger gave to the five bunnies to carry home.

That afternoon, Mr Rabbit carefully chose a sunny patch in the corner of the garden, just right for growing things. With Mrs Rabbit calling out instructions from the gardening book, Mr Rabbit dug the soil with a fork. Then he raked the soil smooth with a rake until the patch of ground was quite ready for sowing. By this time, however, it was late in the afternoon and Mr Rabbit said they would wait until tomorrow to sow the carrot seeds.

'We shall just have to wait for them to grow,' said Mrs Rabbit in despair. And that is what they did.

Every day, Mrs Rabbit went out into the garden with her big, green watering can and watered all the places she could think of where the seeds might be. One day, she found first one, then two, then dozens of tiny seedlings peeping through the flower beds. She looked around the goldfish pond and found some there, too. A little later she saw one fine carrot growing amongst a cluster of bright marigolds and, yet another had rooted itself firmly in the middle of the lawn.

When the carrots were fully grown, everyone agreed that they were quite the best they had ever seen. And, because the bunnies had planted so many seeds, there were enough carrots to feed them for a long, long time.

'Well,' laughed Mrs Rabbit to her five playful bunnies, 'things are not so bad after all. Whenever we need some carrots for supper, all we have to do is look for them. And,' she added, 'playing "Hunt the Carrots" is much more fun than shopping for them!'

The next morning, Mr and Mrs Rabbit were up bright and early. They put on their gardening hats and boots, then looked about for the packets of carrot seeds. 'Now where have those bunnies put them?' said Mrs Rabbit.

She did not have to look for long. Out in the garden she could hear squeals of delight from five excited bunnies. There, skipping and dancing around the garden, the bunnies were sowing the seeds all over the place.

'Oh, my ears!' exclaimed Mrs Rabbit.

'Oh my carrots!' shouted Mr Rabbit, running down the garden path. 'You naughty, wicked bunnies!' he scolded. 'Now, whatever shall we do!'

Well, there was nothing they could do. Tiny little seeds were scattered all over the garden – in amongst the flower beds, behind the bushes, around the goldfish pond – they were everywhere! Everywhere, except in the vegetable patch.

A Home for a Swan

After the snow fell the weather grew colder and colder. Before Tom went out in the mornings his mother helped him to put on his overcoat, scarf, hat, thick gloves and fur-lined boots.

'And keep moving about,' she told him. 'It's far too cold to stand still.'

Tom thought he would go down to the river, to see whether any ice had formed on it yet. There was ice on the farm pond, nearly thick enough to slide on, but the river still flowed, dark and swift. Dad said that he could remember once seeing the river frozen right over.

He trotted through the farmyard, across the orchard and down to the river's edge. Snow had drifted around the reeds at the edge of the water. Prodding with his toe, Tom could feel that there was ice underneath. It creaked and cracked, so he knew it could not be very thick.

Then he heard another sound – a fierce hissing. Suddenly, from among the reeds a long white neck, with a black and yellow beak at the end of it, darted out and only just missed his legs. He moved back quickly and turned to run away, as a huge white bird came floundering out of the reeds.

He ran back to the farmyard. 'Dad,' he cried, 'there's an enormous white bird down by the river, and it nearly pecked me. It's very fierce.'

'I'll come and see it,' said his father.

Taking Tom's hand he walked down with him through the orchard to the river, where they found the great white bird, sprawling among the reeds. It was lying on its breast, with one wing stretched out over the snow.

'It's a swan,' said Tom's Dad.

'He's hurt, isn't he?' asked Tom.

'Yes, I think he has a broken wing,' said his father.

They went to get some other men to help them catch the swan. They had to splash about in the cold water at the edge of the river, as the swan tried to escape. When they had caught it they wrapped a sack around it, to keep it from struggling. Then two of them carried the bird back to the farm, while another held its neck to stop it from pecking.

Dad telephoned the vet, who came and bound up the wing with a bandage.

'I think he had better live with the geese,' said Dad.

So for the rest of the winter the six geese had the swan for company. At first he was very wild and savage, but after a

time he settled down and seemed to enjoy his life in the farm-yard. Dad called him Cygnus, because he said that was an old name for a swan. They fed him with barley meal and grains of corn every day.

After many weeks the vet came to take off the bandages. Cygnus stretched his wings and shook himself. Then he flapped his wings. The injured one had healed.

Cygnus stayed till the end of winter. Then, one afternoon when the primroses were in bloom and the grass was growing green again, Tom heard a whooping noise overhead. He looked up and was just in time to see Cygnus circling around like a giant white aeroplane. He watched the swan clear the tops of the apple trees and then make off over the meadows towards the south.

Tom felt sad.

'I don't suppose we shall see Cygnus again,' he said.

'I don't expect so,' said his mother.

But Dad said, 'I wonder!' and he sat there, thinking.

The next winter, when the frost and ice came again, Dad looked at the dark, cloudy sky and said, 'I think we shall have snow.'

Tom looked up at the clouds. 'There's a flake or two falling now!' he exclaimed.

'So there is,' said Dad, holding out his hand and catching a snow-flake.

Then Tom cried, 'Oh, look!'

Wheeling down out of the sky with the snow-flakes were five birds. They circled above and then came down slowly and landed on the river among the reeds. They soon paddled to the shore and came walking through the orchard towards the farm.

Cygnus led the way. With him was a smaller white swan. She was his mate. And after them came their young – three soft brown swans.

They all went straight to the goose-pen and settled down inside.

'Well!' said Tom. 'Cygnus has come home for the winter, and brought his family with him.'

Bimbo's Night in the Wood

'Squirrel,' called Badger, peering up through the leaves of a big old tree. 'Are you there?' Bimbo, the budgie, sat perched on Badger's shoulder.

After a few moments, they caught sight of a bushy red tail.

'Badger!' exclaimed Squirrel, landing on a low branch. 'What a lovely surprise! Who's your tired little friend?'

he went on, pointing to Bimbo, who was swaying sleepily on Badger's shoulder.

'This is Bimbo,' replied Badger. 'He's had a very busy day out visiting and would like somewhere to sleep tonight so that he'll be fresh to fly home in the morning.'

'Leave it all to me, Badger,' said Squirrel. 'I'll look after you, Bimbo.'

Bimbo fluttered up to the branch beside Squirrel, who suddenly took a flying leap and landed in the next tree. 'Follow me,' he called, as he scampered up to the top of the tree. There, hidden amongst the leaves, was an empty nest.

'It's very comfortable,' said Bimbo, settling down. Soon he was fast asleep.

'Tu-whit, tu-whoo,' called an owl in the middle of the night. 'Sorry . . . I was just telling Squirrel you were safe.'

'How kind!' replied Bimbo.

The little budgie was up with the sun next morning. He called on all his new woodland friends and said goodbye sadly. Then, remembering how worried Amanda would be, he took to the air, and with one last wave to the little group down below, he left the wood behind.

You will find the first story about Bimbo the budgerigar on page 20.